HUNTING HANDSOME ROB

A HANDSOME ROB GIG

BLAZE WARD

KNOTTED ROAD PRESS

ALSO BY BLAZE WARD

The Handsome Rob Gigs

Can't Shoot Straight Gang

Can't Shoot Straight Gang Returns

Hunting Handsome Rob

The Jessica Keller Chronicles

Auberon

Queen of the Pirates

Last of the Immortals

Goddess of War

Flight of the Blackbird

The Red Admiral

St. Legier

Winterhome

Petron

CS-405

Queen Anne's Revenge

Packmule

Persephone

Additional Alexandria Station Stories

Siren

Two Bottles of Wine with a War God

The Story Road

The Science Officer Series

The Science Officer

The Mind Field

The Gilded Cage

The Pleasure Dome

The Doomsday Vault

The Last Flagship

The Hammerfield Gambit

The Hammerfield Payoff

Shadow of the Dominion

Longshot Hypothesis

Hard Bargain

Outermost

Dominion-427

Phoenix

Princess Rualoh

Earth Force Sky Patrol

Birth of the Star Dragon

Flight of the Star Dragon

Call of the Star Dragon

Shadow of the Star Dragon

Trial of the Star Dragon

1

____

THE SOUND OF SOMETHING SLAMMING HARD INTO THE front door of his apartment woke Handsome Rob from a dead sleep.

He'd gone to bed reasonably sober, and close enough to a decent hour, at least for him. Someone apparently wasn't fond of waiting for the morning, to deliver whatever message needed saying at…three fourteen in the morning.

First try must have surprised them. Probably expecting to go right through his door. The door Nigel had quietly upgraded when nobody was looking.

Second blow against the door was harder. Enough that he might have even heard it dead drunk.

Rob exploded into action, pistol in one hand from under the other pillow of his queen-sized bed.

The Service had warned him this day might come. A guy in his industry made lots of enemies, and eventually one of them was going to find you. Probably time to disappear from Puerto Peñasco altogether and start living out of temporary digs, somewhere else on the planet, where his name never appeared on the lease, like most of his compatriots.

Assuming he was still alive by the time the sun came up.

Into pants and a warm pullover shirt. Wallet, handcomm, holster. Small tactical bag Nigel had always insisted rest near the bed, for exactly this sort of emergency. Jacket, because it had been drizzling earlier and things were going to get ugly soon.

Somebody had finally brought up something heavier for the front door to his apartment, after kicking it in didn't work and shooting the handle and the lock just killed one of the five bolts holding the beast shut.

At Jorge's insistence, Rob had pretty much blackmailed his bosses, *The Lincolnshire Guardia Civil Interior*, also known as 'The Service,' into upgrading the whole front wall along the hallway with some hull metal that the navy would never miss. Right now, nothing handheld would penetrate the wall, but the door could still be blown off its hinges.

Third shot of something looked to be doing a reasonable job of attempting that.

Rob owed Nigel big for this one, since that crazy redneck had designed the system. Someone had been planning to kick his door in and bums rush the bedroom, catching him passed out or at least getting to him before he could do anything.

Handsome Rob was on autopilot by now, letting his training and reflexes handle things. Roberto Segura. Six-foot-one. One-ninety-five. Black eyes. Black hair. Hispanic genotype.

At least the last five were accurate enough for government work.

He went into the closet and grabbed a coat hook with his off hand, pistol still aimed at the door where trouble might yet come through.

At least nobody had decided to come in through the windows as part of the initial attack. Those were also reinforced, but if someone had brought that level of trouble, he'd already be under observation and maybe hostile fire from outside right now.

Small miracles.

A section of the back wall puffed slightly and withdrew in response to the coat hook-disguised lever. Not much, just enough that Rob could step in and onto a claustrophobic ladder down, pausing to push the wall section back into place with a click once he was clear.

They'd probably figure it out pretty quickly when he disappeared, especially if they were tracking his electronics, which he assumed they were at this point. Still, it had been Nigel's idea, cutting into a ventilation shaft for the whole building and installing a ladder that got Rob to the basement.

Safely down three flights, he opened a panel on hinges that Nigel had put in. After some wriggling, he got clear, stepping out into a laundry room. His greatest fear had been that someone would get to the top of the shaft before he got out the bottom, firing pistols or tossing some stun grenades down.

It would have been like shooting fish in a barrel at that point, with him as the fish.

Rob crossed the room and opened the locker he kept down here, where Nigel had stashed a larger tactical bag. More of an overnight bag, in case he needed to run like hell without ever coming back to his apartment.

Like now.

Someone kicking in the front door with enough firepower to do the job wasn't an angry boyfriend of some woman he'd seduced.

Probably.

Unless they'd all gotten together and decided to make it a team play.

There weren't that many of them, were there?

Rob shook his head and pulled a knit cap from the bag, drawing it on and adding gloves. Nigel's small bag got emptied and put into the locker, so Rob had gear in pockets, pouches, and places.

Nigel might be crazy, but that boy believed in being prepared.

Rob slung the larger bag, really just big enough for a pair of dress shoes, but compact, and headed for the locked door down a half-flight of stairs in the corner.

This building had been part of a quad when it was built, a century ago. Underground tunnels had connected them, so folks didn't have to go out into the withering summer heat, or the current winter rains, to get around.

Two of the four buildings had since been sold off and torn down, but the tunnels still ran under one of them.

Rob knew how to pick locks, but Roxy had found him a key, so he was able to open the door and step through, pulling it shut behind him. Enough emergency lights still worked down here so that he could see where he was going, and anything that moved was likely to get shot with the gun he still carried in one hand.

The only person he might apologize to would be a possum that had somehow gotten into the building.

Under the building, across the street, and up to an emergency evacuation stairwell next to a deli/coffee shop that had the good sense to be closed at this hour. Maybe he'd need to find a donut shop soon, though. Felt like it was going to be a long night.

He'd walked this scenario enough times with members of the team that the Service referred to informally as the *Can't Shoot Straight Gang* for his actions to be automatic, but he'd never imagined that he would actually be here.

Still, training was training. You did these things so that they became automatic in an emergency.

Tonight felt like an emergency.

At the top of the stair, he pressed on the handle enough to release the latch and cracked the door no more than a few centimeters.

Darkness.

His apartment was on a third floor corner, but he couldn't see it from here without opening this door far enough to stick his head out, so he just assumed he was blown at this point.

Some traffic on the street. Early morning workers going in or out, depending. Night owls who'd had a bite to eat after the clubs closed. Something.

Rob took a deep breath and slipped out the door, closing it silently as he got clear.

Cities are not dark at night, so he was wearing a gray jacket and blue dungarees that were faded enough to vanish against concrete or marble, where black would stand out like an inkspot.

Again, know your surroundings and be prepared for them.

He just wasn't supposed to ever need this.

The bookstore was dark, so he slipped into the doorwell for a moment and pulled out his handcomm.

Assume you are blown, and they are tracking you.

That was the training for this situation, reinforced from Jorge all the way down to Longbow.

Rather than call it in to headquarters, he dialed Roxy's personal number and stepped out from his hiding space as a vegetable truck trundled down the street, probably headed to the green grocer three blocks over.

Rob stepped to the corner just as the truck stopped but before it had started to turn.

Quietly, he tossed the handcomm into the back of the flatbed, landing it on a box of asparagus, if he was seeing the shapes right.

Someone tracking him via comm signal would be going the wrong way, and possibly scare the hell out of a bunch of civilians in a few minutes when they caught up.

He'd be long gone, assuming no watchers on the streets recognized him, hunched over some and walking like a half-drunk man.

He crossed behind the truck, then crossed again, heading inland rather than down towards the water. Whatever was happening, he needed to be away from the scene, and to do it without even a memory of him having been here.

There weren't many places someone could get his personal address. Unless someone inside the Service had tipped them off.

Assume you can't come in from the cold, if it gets that bad. Go to ground and only rely on people you personally know and trust, until you know what happened.

He was in Puerto Peñasco on *Ramsey*. Supposedly between missions and enjoying a well-earned month off, after saving the galaxy again. Or at least *Lincolnshire*.

Had the pirates figured out who he was? Or paid someone enough cash for a file to get copied and then lost?

Behind him, an explosion caused Rob to slip into another doorway and look back.

Bastards had just blown up his apartment, spraying the block back there with plexiglass and possibly all his furniture.

Rob growled under his breath, pulled his cap down, took a deep, angry breath, then kept moving.

Nothing in that apartment he'd miss, except the memories. All his important papers were kept in a safety deposit box downtown, where he couldn't get to them for two and a half days, when they opened on Monday.

He just had to stay alive long enough to sort it all out.

Buses were running this late, but it wasn't that far of a walk, and he'd need the exercise to burn off all the adrenaline. Plus, he didn't want to be trapped in a civilian vehicle if whoever just blew up his life decided to continue the hunt and got lucky.

He slipped into the shadows again, crossed an alley with the pistol down by his side where he could snap-shoot someone, and moved through the night.

2

———

Rob walked through the door and looked around carefully, having tromped the five kilometers to the Sonora district through alleys and side streets. Then down a half-staircase and into a below-street dive, two blocks from El Ayuntamiento.

In the wrong direction. The bad direction.

Of course, anybody deciding to mug him tonight, as keyed up as Rob was, had already decided that they were tired of life and looking for a painful way out.

He got in and quick-scanned the interior as he walked to a stool well away from everyone still around at this time of night.

Morning?

The tables and booths were all empty, which he'd feared, but prepared for.

Tallia was working bar tonight instead of waitressing, so he took a spot at the long, oak bar, well away from the other three folks who didn't look like they wanted to go home.

She started to smile when she saw him, but Rob glared at her and shook his head, ever so slightly.

Instantly, Tallia's face went gruff and bored. She wandered this way in a sideways manner, keeping an eye on her other three drunks.

"What'll it be?" she asked flatly.

"Highball of tequila," Rob said sourly.

She nodded and turned her back, grabbing a bottle and pouring. Tallia twisted and slid it across to him. Her eyes shone with the faintest recognition that he was working.

Rob grabbed it and sniffed. Sure enough. Top shelf stuff rather than the industrial crap they served dockers and office drones.

He nodded as she drifted away and took a sip.

Tallia wasn't part of the Service, but Jorge Royo was. He owned this bar, as well as the building it was contained in. And several other places.

Claimed it was a fantastic way to easily launder the money the Service paid him under the table for some of the crazy missions he ran, while he was right up front about being one of the most famous actors in the sector.

As Jorge said, with enough audacity, you can do anything, and nobody will ever believe the truth.

Tallia was a civilian, but she knew enough, and was smart enough, to not blow his cover here if he didn't want her to.

He drank a little and tried to calm his nerves.

The place had seemed safe enough, scouting it from an alley across the way. Little traffic, this late at night, and nobody he had recognized.

Walking in had been a calculated risk, but he was armed. Probably keyed up enough that he would end up apologizing to a possum for shooting it in some alleyway by the time he was done.

These things happened.

Jorge was off-planet. Something about a celebrity golf tournament somewhere. Longbow was deep into a recording studio with his new band, having spent the month since they got home polishing up what the man claimed might be an album almost as good as the original Longbow album that had catapulted Levi Framingham into the stratosphere of rock gods. Right before a car wreck during his first tour that effectively ended his career and turned him into a spy.

Sort of.

Part of Jorge's team, like the rest of them. Cover identity as himself, at least a different version of himself. Maybe one where he could be happy finally.

Rob wasn't about to bring all his troubles to the man's doorstep. Not unless he had to.

Tallia wandered back after checking on her three drunks. Rob nursed the glass a little more, then dug out a couple of coins. Jorge never charged him for the booze, but he couldn't be paying her that well.

Could he?

Best not to push.

She got close and leaned on the back of the bar in such a way that her cleavage was distracting. He was pretty sure Jorge was the only one she had eyes for, but he appreciated the effort to brighten things.

"You look like a man having a bad day," she said in a quiet, off-hand way.

"Worse than bad," Rob growled back, aware that they might have an audience. "Wish there was something somebody could do, but I'm on my own."

Tallia's eyes got a shrouded look in them. She knew who he normally ran with, so she'd get the reference. And understand that she probably didn't want his problems.

Rob didn't even know who was after him, which just made it worse. Even Tallia was a calculated risk of a contact, but Jorge trusted her. If she had somehow been turned, they were all in trouble.

"We don't close," Tallia mentioned off-hand. "Staff will be in and light the kitchen up in a little while. Would hot food help?"

Rob considered it, but he needed to keep moving. Plus, anybody who knew his personal address just might be able to guess he'd end up here. Best if he just passed through.

"Moving on," he said as he finished the glass and slid off the back of the stool. "If I'm not here, my troubles can't find me."

Tallia nodded just enough for him to notice, and then grabbed the empty, wiped the bar, and watched him depart in silence.

At least she'd be able to pass a message along. Jorge wouldn't be back for a while, but he might have left emergency contact information.

As far as Rob knew, he was the only person on his team on planet, not counting Longbow.

Time to move.

He needed to stay ahead of whoever was hunting him.

At least until he could turn the tables on them.

3

———

The comm unit next to the bed ringing woke
Miguel. That was never good. The clock suggested that dawn
was not far off.

Miguel grabbed it after the second ring, but Caroline still
stirred.

"I have it, dear," he said, sitting up and pulling the
handset to his ear. "Hello?"

The system chirped at him, rather than a human
speaking.

An even worse sign.

Miguel reached into the drawer and pulled out a device
he slipped over the handset and activated. The two systems
warbled at each other for a moment and then fell silent.

"Cabrill, M. Oh-Six-Nine-Four-Four-One," he said into
the now-scrambled comm.

"We have a situation," the man at the other end replied
simply.

Stansfield Brightmeadow-Gates, his Staff Chief. The
person all emergencies would eventually route to, until
Brightmeadow-Gates decided that something was bad

13

enough to rouse the head of the Service well before his normal alarm clock.

"Go ahead," Miguel replied.

"Police and fire are responding to an explosion and fire at an address belonging to one of our agents," the man said in that dry, severe voice he affected when he wanted to look down that long nose of his at the *Cowboys* over in the Operations Inspectorate.

"Where?" Miguel demanded quietly.

"The unit is located here in Puerto Peñasco," Brightmeadow-Gates said. "It belongs to Segura."

Ah. Handsome Rob. One of Brightmeadow-Gates's least favorite agents, Especially since the man had managed to pull off the impossible twice now, using methods that were the exact opposite of what Brightmeadow-Gates felt was correct field craft. The patient, quiet kind.

"Do we know anything at this point?" Miguel asked, standing up and pulling the blanket back up before Caroline had to stir because she was cold.

"No," came the reply. "Automated communications traffic picked it up, flagged it, and routed it to Alcazar's people. He reviewed the log and called me. Given the sensitivity of some of Segura's recent escapades, I felt it was worth waking you up, Miguel."

Yes, that would be a good call. Segura might not be aware of some of the enemies he had made, both among the ranks of Lincolnshire's enemies, as well as within their own government.

Miguel considered things for a moment and came to a decision.

"Have them send my car around in about thirty minutes," he said. "And tell whoever's behind the wheel to hit the drive-through on the way, so I have a hot breakfast and fresh coffee as we come in. Activate the war room, just in case, and have Alcazar and a team ready to brief me in an hour or so."

"Very good," Brightmeadow-Gates acknowledged and hung up.

Miguel did the same, detaching the scrambler and slipping it into the drawer.

"Problems?" Caroline rolled over just enough to look at him without losing any of the heat under the quilt.

"Probably nothing, dear," Miguel smiled at her, however thin it might be.

He considered things for a moment.

"Still, perhaps we should reschedule dinner with the Garcias," Miguel continued after a moment.

That got an eyebrow raised at him, but it couldn't be helped.

"I'm sure I'm an old hen who's overreacting," he continued.

"Rarely," Caroline replied sagely. "Who is it?"

"One of Jorge's people might be having a spot of trouble," Miguel said.

He had remarkably few secrets from the woman, but that was the nature of the business, being the man in charge of Lincolnshire's entire espionage service.

"Handsome?" she asked.

Miguel nodded, concerned.

It would be unfortunate if that young man had to pay the piper.

4

THE CAR WAS WAITING OUT FRONT. MIGUEL EMERGED, looking carefully in all directions. He had never been an agent, but had been through enough training to have added their paranoia to his own.

The sun was lightening the eastern sky, but only in an off-hand, drowsy kind of way that suggested he would be in the office before it came time to draw the shades. Except he'd be downstairs as soon as he arrived, listening to hard young men and women barking back and forth at each other in a coded dialect that was frequently too dense for outsiders like him to penetrate.

But that was later. Right now, he had two breakfast sandwiches on English muffins and a mug of coffee waiting for him. That would get him to lunch, and by then they should have a better understanding of the situation.

Hopefully, it would be resolved positively by then, but Miguel had an uneasy feeling in the pit of his stomach. Like perhaps they had all been on too good of a run lately.

He ate as they rode.

The Service itself was housed in a set of mundane brick

blocks not that far from the river. From the outside, it always reminded Miguel of the headquarters of a particularly successful accounting firm. Not as reserved as an insurance conglomerate, but lacking the flash of anything more interesting. Most of those sorts of industries eventually moved into some hideous construct that tended to reflect the ego of the man or woman in charge.

He supposed the same could have been said about the Service, had any outsiders known the truth, but on *Ramsey*, there was only a limited clientele for the product his organization produced, so they didn't have to have High Street flash.

That was why people like Jorge Royo were on the payroll, after all. And, after Jorge finally made retirement stick in a few years, Handsome Rob would hopefully be in a position to carry that torch forward.

If he survived that long.

Breakfast was gone and being digested just as the car entered the underground garage designed to hide their secrets. Miguel popped out of the back as the car rolled to a stop next to Stansfield on the curb, standing like a headmaster awaiting some pupil's parents for a good discussion of better decorum than they had instilled in their own child previously.

Miguel understood the group that Stansfield Brightmeadow-Gates always derided as *The Cowboys on Three*, since their office was down on that floor. You needed the Operations Inspectorate when Data Analysis and Signals Intelligence failed. Most of the time, they weren't even cowboys, those men and women.

Handsome Rob was in a rather special category. *When all else has failed.*

Miguel would miss the boy, if he'd gotten himself killed.

Another anonymous star on the wall in the canteen, reminding everyone that this was not just another office job.

"Any update?" Miguel asked after they had passed through the second secured door and he could be reasonably sure that they were contained.

"None, as yet," Stansfield replied disapprovingly.

Miguel nodded and they entered the War Room.

Operations Central, usually only activated when there was a major counter-intelligence operation in progress against what were normally *Salonnian* spies, although every nation had been caught with their hands in the cookie jar more than once.

Dolf met them inside the glass-walled control room that looked over the bay and his dozen or so staff, all busy at work.

Rudolfo Alcazar, Chief of the Operations Inspectorate.

The head *Cowboy*.

The man looked like Central Casting had sent him over. Tall and muscular, even for a man in his early fifties. Brown hair with just a touch of gray at the edges. Bright blue eyes that always had an eagle quality about them. Charming in a gruff, masculine way that usually caused women to go into a sort of quiet, sexual overdrive that Miguel had never really understood.

But he knew enough to put the man into the slot, where Dolf used his powers as frequently on female politicians with budgetary authority as he once had on *Aquitaine* agents, if the rumors were true.

"Dolf," Miguel greeted the man and got a firm handshake as Stansfield nodded at the door and left him.

Brightmeadow-Gates would head up to Six and handle the paperwork and meetings while Miguel sat down here and followed the situation.

"Status?" Miguel asked as he found himself a seat with a view and sat his coffee down on a side table.

Dolf would pace. He did that. Miguel expected it.

"Esmeralda's folks caught a sniff early on," Dolf said, referring to the Data Analysis Inspectorate that was in charge of all the electronic monitoring . The sort of thing that was the meat and potatoes of an intelligence agency. "She routed it over with a flag, since she knew it was one of ours, and our special boy, that might have gotten into trouble."

Miguel nodded.

"Emergency services got there after an explosion was reported," Dolf continued. "Reinforced concrete and steel building, so not much that could burn, and the fire was out pretty quickly. No bodies were located."

"Have you invoked the Emergency Secrets Act?" Miguel asked.

That was within Dolf's power, just barely, given the circumstances.

"I have not," the man stopped pacing and fixed Miguel with a glare. "Eye-witness accounts suggested someone tried to break the door down before the explosion. Apparently succeeded. Then they blew the place apart. But Rob wasn't there when the police arrived."

"You still could have invoked," Miguel said carefully.

"If they were going after Rob Segura, then we have a larger problem, Miguel," Dolf replied. "Such as, how did they know where and how to find him?"

"Has one of his enemies caught up with him?"

"Not without help," Dolf started pacing again. "Our help, for whatever it's worth."

"Understood," Miguel said.

If Dolf Alcazar was suggesting a mole giving outsiders information, then the Service indeed had larger problems.

Miguel considered his options. This was why they'd rousted him, once certain ramifications became clear.

"I will invoke the Emergency Secrets Act for you, Dolf," Miguel said. "Put teams out to discover if Segura was taken, or managed to escape and has gone into hiding. I'll notify the Minister and see to it that she knows enough to deflect others, without putting her in an awkward position later. Have you notified the rest of Segura's team that they might be at risk?"

"The *Can't Shoot Straight Gang* are mostly off-planet right now," Dolf said. "I checked. Jorge is at an event, with Phipps acting as his gopher. Mrs. Jones is at a combat training resort for her annual recertifications. Only Framingham is local, but he's half a planet away in Lincoln or Landing, apparently recording an album with the folks Royo and Segura brought back from the most recent mission."

"Alert Longbow directly, just in case, and then have an extra security team added to whatever he has now," Miguel ordered. "Quietly, mind you. If you're suggesting a leak, we'll need to keep this close to the vest for now. The team doesn't need to know anything other than to be extra careful for a bit."

"Understood, Miguel," Dolf said. "More concerned about Handsome for now. Framingham is far more dangerous than he looks. Or lets on."

"And we haven't heard anything from Rob?" Miguel asked.

"We have not," Dolf said. "That concerns me more."

5

————

R OB WAS PRETTY SURE HE'D LEFT THE BAR CLEAN, BUT
he'd still picked up a tail of some sort. He felt eyes on the
back of his head when he walked, but couldn't trip them up
into revealing themselves.

Nobody was tracking him by his handcomm. That
should have led whoever it was to the grocery, where they
would awkwardly stumble into a group of civilians
unpacking boxes of vegetables.

The sun would be up soon, but not that soon. He had
another hour or two before traffic on the streets and
sidewalks would be sufficient for him to just vanish into. The
only people about now were the tardy night owls getting
home from a Friday night, early morning runners, and a few
people headed in to whatever shift duty called on them to be
bright-eyed and bushy-tailed at way-too-early in the
morning. Restaurants and donut shops, he supposed.

Maybe ten people in sight, total.

Rob made it a point to never get up that early unless he
had to. More likely, he'd have still been going at this point,

after a night of dancing and unsuccessful seductions. The kind where he didn't get breakfast in the bargain.

There.

Movement, back a block and across the street. Someone ducking into an alley, or ducking back when he turned around. But still following for several blocks now it felt.

Whoever it was, they were too far away for him to risk a physical confrontation. This felt like someone who had been part of a third ring of surveillance, and Rob had just gotten unlucky enough to be spotted.

Which suggested that they knew what he looked like.

Like maybe it wasn't a fluke that someone had tried to kick in his door, and had settled for blowing up his flat.

That also meant the someone was probably calling for help right now. Vectoring trouble down onto him while he dithered.

Always move quickly. A decent plan now beats a perfect plan tomorrow. You are a shark. Swim fast or drown.

Rob had forgotten who told him that, but it didn't really matter. Good advice.

He took it, breaking into a hard jog as he reached a corner and turned sharply away from the person who might have only been a shy walker, or someone stopping to take a piss in an anonymous alley.

Rob didn't believe it for a moment. This was when all the usual workouts would come into play. The ability to run a half-marathon at the drop of a hat, mostly because he hadn't been out all night dancing.

For once.

Even moving at a fast jog, his shoes made hardly any noise. More training, this from Roxy, of all people. But she was probably the most dangerous agent he had ever met, so learn from the best, just as he bought the same aftershave as Jorge did.

Every car was a risk now. When would a window suddenly roll down for a man or a woman with a bolter to start spraying fire at him?

Rob had no idea who might be after him. Didn't matter. The only thing on his list right now was survival. Getting out of the immediate kill radius of whatever teams had brought the big guns after him.

He considered pulling out the burner comm and calling for help as he slashed across a street and through a ground floor shopping arcade that wouldn't have even the coffee shop open for another hour.

Something stayed his hand as he started to reach.

How had they known where to find him?

The apartment was unlisted. The Service held the lease through one of their holding companies.

Handsome Rob should still be invisible.

But there were watchers on the street.

Behind him. Rob heard a vehicle suddenly land hard from repulsors, onto the skids with that grinding sound you got when the driver decided to bleed off momentum on the asphalt rather than taking the extra moment to come to a stop.

The sound of doors opening and closing carried through the strange acoustics of the arcade like they were parked right next to him instead of sixty meters away.

Rob stretched his stride, letting the hand holding the pistol start pumping, rather than staying down on his thigh where a casual witness might not realize he was armed.

Those folks back there weren't casual.

Rob reached the top of a flight of stairs that would split traffic several ways. He got down several steps and hazarded a look back.

Shadows were just entering the open space over there.

Several of them. The lights weren't bright enough to see anything but shapes, but the intent was obvious.

Just to make a point, Rob snapped two shots off at them. He wasn't trying to hit, and assumed they had body armor on, which he did not.

This was just setting the stakes. If these were the same people, they'd already kicked in his door and blown up his apartment.

They went to cover with quick barks of orders, rather than panic that Rob might have expected from a group of insurance salesmen getting home late from all-night sushi and karaoke.

Rob ducked and turned as the folks over there cut loose with pulse rifles. Quieter than bolters or other slug-throwing implements. Faster to lose efficacy over range, as well.

Just about the perfect weapon if you wanted to play ninja games in the middle of a city, as Friday night finally gave up and allowed Saturday morning to think about rousting itself from bed.

He hit the bottom of the steps, turned into a corridor that went under the street, and ran.

6

———

Lost them.

At least Rob was pretty sure he had.

It had been touch and go for a bit.

That bastard in the repulsorlift sedan had dropped his cargo and then immediately started running squares in the area, presumably calling back to the men on foot if he saw anything.

It would have been easier for the driver to spot Handsome Rob had he taken off, but hovering over one spot for very long would have made him show up on a sensor, and cops would have come over to see what was going on. None of the beam fire this morning had probably been loud enough to wake someone up, so the authorities might have missed it all.

Maybe next time he should pack the loudest slugthrower Nigel could find or modify.

Rob would have appreciated a little police intervention right about now, but all his training was strict about not showing up on official channels unless he had to.

Hopefully, friendlies back at headquarters had picked up the troubles by now and were waiting for him to call in.

Rob would have called already, but couldn't rid himself of the fear that the first person he called would make a second call, letting their friends back there know where to find him.

He was beginning to understand why Jorge was only willing to contract with the Service on as-needed and as-available footing. Only taking the jobs he wanted, and controlling everything his way. But Jorge was already rich enough that he could afford to sit around in a bar all day with a bottomless martini glass in one hand.

Nobody loved Handsome Rob that much yet.

At least not until Longbow released his new album and Rob would be due a part of a producer slice. Jorge had suggested that the residuals might buy Rob his own bar.

He just had to stay alive long enough to collect it.

Rob was across the street from a park now. A good one, with lots of trees and brush, designed more to mimic wildlife habitat than just being a perfectly level pitch of green for picnics and pickup rugby matches.

Places to hide. Places to run. Places to watch.

Fortunately, it felt like they'd only been chasing him, so far, rather than herding a lone agent into a kill zone, but he still paused and studied the terrain over there.

Shadows that could hide assassins just as well as assignations. Picnics, hand-overs, and trysts.

Whatever trouble a guy like Handsome Rob might get into on a Tuesday afternoon in the summer, when the sun was warm and the breeze was perfect.

Too bad she'd gone off and gotten married to a mechanic.

Rob looked both ways with a wistfulness of regret and bolted across the street as fast as his legs would carry him.

No shots rang out. No beams reached out from the darkness ahead of him or behind him. Rob hit the first cluster of bushes with his free hand out and the pistol tight against his side, expecting someone to stand suddenly and open fire or swing at him with a samurai sword.

Or whatever the fight choreographer had decided would make a great scene at this point in the script.

Nothing.

He squatted down and turned to look behind him, but the alley he'd come out of was quiet, and the traffic on the street was still mostly one-shot vehicles headed somewhere.

Good enough.

Rob slipped deeper into the brush, wondering if he could chance any of his professional contacts, or if this needed to be kept outside.

Nigel had left him a burner handcomm that he could use. Rob pulled it out and dialed a number he had long-since memorized.

7

THE VOICES BARKING CAUSED MIGUEL TO LOOK UP FROM the report he'd been reading.

"Repeat that," Dolf called over the noise of people.

"Got an incoming call," a woman said. "Claims to be Segura."

"Put it on conference here in the control room and everybody else listen in," Dolf said after looking over at Miguel for a nod.

A beep and the room had that extra ambiance that it got when there was an open comm line.

"Talk to me," Dolf called out, eyes up at the ceiling like people did.

"Segura, R. Two-Five-Three-Seven-One-One," a voice replied quietly.

Miguel looked over at the man in the corner and got the man's nod of confirmation. Dolf heaved a quiet sigh of relief.

"It's Dolf," he said. "Where are you?"

"Gone rabbit," Segura replied. "Got low trust right now. Pack of dogs on my tail with heavy weapons and professional support."

"Understood, Rob," Dolf tried to sound placating.

Miguel stood now and walked over to where he could look over a shoulder at the young man typing furiously on his keyboard. Miguel didn't understand the esoteric graphics display, except that the man seemed to be tracking backwards through far more transmission towers that he should have needed to, even to reach this building.

What had Rob said? *Low trust*.

So, he didn't think this was a secure line. And obviously wasn't using a unit issued by the Research and Development Inspectorate. Miguel had an image of Nigel Phipps, smiling the way that man did when he wanted to put one over on the boffins.

"What can we do to help, Rob?" Dolf was asking behind Miguel.

He turned and Dolf was gesturing to the others in the room to get the trace completed.

"I'm in Hidalgo Park now, but moving," Rob replied.

Miguel heard the noises of a man standing and moving through brush, perhaps.

"Can't stay here long, because I only have a small head start on whoever," Rob's voice got almost too quiet for the microphone to pick up. "There's a donut shop on Ninth that should be about open by the time I can get there."

"I know the place, Rob," Dolf said. "You want heavy teams or just a pickup?"

"Just a pickup," Rob said after a moment. "Low key. Pretty sure I've lost them, but they'd notice a team moving downtown. Won't be enough traffic in the vicinity to mask friendlies moving around for another hour or ninety minutes."

"I'll send a Service car," Dolf said. "Once we get you in, we can figure out what happened."

"Thanks, boss," Rob said, and then he abruptly cut the line.

Looking over the other agent's shoulder, they had finally cut through the redirections that the device was using, and had isolated it to the south end of Hidalgo Park, just like expected.

Miguel took a deep breath and made sure his face was calm and jovial by the time he turned around to the rest of the room.

"Sounds like you've got everything in hand, Dolf." Miguel walked over and smiled at Dolf. "I'll head upstairs and start the forensics investigations we'll need. Keep me posted."

"Will do," Dolf said, turning his attention to the team around him as Miguel exited the War Room and decided to take the stairs today.

He needed a few extra minutes to think before he emerged upstairs. Being out of breath from the climb would be a good enough cover for now.

Segura had started the conversation by indicating *low trust* in his surroundings. Miguel had read enough debriefing reports to understand that to be a technical term the agents used.

A suggestion of deeper problems or unknown watchers compromising communications.

Yet, in the very next breath, Segura had laid out his itinerary and asked for only a single vehicle to arrive and pick him up, when the present situation could be easily stretched to drop every heavy assault team on call in a box around the man as a way of protecting him.

Dolf had missed that, in his excitement at getting his agent safe, perhaps. Miguel had not.

It didn't add up. As Miguel started climbing out of the basement, his fifty-four-year-old legs complained, having spent perhaps too much time seated at a desk, rather than on the treadmill.

Unless Handsome Rob suspected that an assassin would somehow be monitoring communications with the Service, and able to get there first.

Which suggested that Segura didn't trust Dolf, or at least the operational security around headquarters.

Maybe he was an old, wet, hen right now, sputtering and over-reacting, but Miguel had a feeling that something would go terribly wrong at that donut shop. Rob was probably expecting it, but who else in the building might?

Worse, if everything did add up, who was listening and telling the bad guys how to find his agent?

Everyone in here was supposedly cleared at the highest levels.

Did he truly have a mole inside the organization?

8

———

Dodger got the radio piece out of his ear and pulled up a buzzing handcomm that had been stashed in his thigh pouch.

They'd lost Segura.

Bastard was just too wily, even for a *Lincolnshire* agent.

Dodger checked the incoming number and grunted, gesturing the men around him into cover and stillness.

"Yeah?" he growled when the line opened.

"Your target will be at a coffee shop at Ninth and Academy sometime in the next twenty-five minutes," an electronically-masked voice said. "He has called for a Service sedan pickup, rather than backup team. This will be your last chance to get him."

"Understood," Dodger said with a grimace as the line went dead.

He and the boys'd already screwed this op pretty badly. The front door had held them long enough for that smarmy bastard to get away from them somehow.

Setting off a shaped charge in the bedroom to cover up evidence wasn't going to hide the fact that they'd broken in.

No, all that did was make it impossible to get any DNA or anything that could be used to identify members of his team later. Defensive measures after the fact rather than success.

Roberto Segura had still given them the slip.

Worse, he'd done it three more times, when the man was supposed to just be another pretty boy agent. The kind with a closet full of tailored tuxedos in various colors that had probably burned pretty damned well, along with everything else. The one that all the girls swooned at, going home with him and whispering all their secrets on a pillow.

Nobody would ever accuse Dodger of being pretty. Unless you thought a twenty-two-pound maul was an attractive thing. Then he might be in the running.

He didn't do nice. He did violent. Extravagant.

Deniable at a later date, when someone needed something done, and didn't need it showing up on quarterly reports as anything but an invoice for services.

Dodger gestured the other three to come out of hiding and step close. Four-man-team. They'd been with him for a while now. No pretty boys here, either. Just rude bruisers that might have gone on to a life of crime.

A bigger life of crime, maybe, since what they did meant jail time if they were ever caught, especially as they could never reveal who they did it for.

"Rabbit's headed north from here," Dodger said as they all squatted down and Dodger put his earpiece back in so he could talk to the car.

They'd tracked Segura to the park, but lost him. Too much cover.

And Pretty Boy was better than they'd been led to believe.

"Swede, Ninth and Academy in twenty minutes," Dodger said. "Meet us on the south side of the park now."

The driver chirped and Dodger looked at the others.

"There's little cover when he gets close, so we'll find a nice spot for a high-powered rifle shot."

One of his boys leaned in and had the fire in his eyes.

"It's a long shot, but there's an office building off Tenth that should have a clear field of fire if we get up on the roof," he said with a savage grin. "Next to the bank."

"Yeah, that'll do," Dodger said, remembering the place. "Shooting someone in that parking lot will bring the authorities, so we'll leave the pulse rifles in the car and just take the sniper and pistols. Car will be on the backside for a leisurely getaway."

The other three nodded and Dodger rose, slipping into the brush silently as their car came to rest at the curb not far away.

Segura might have had all the luck of the gods up until now, but they'd catch him just when he probably thought he'd given them the slip.

And then *BANG*, one less *Cowboy* in the world.

9

Given his druthers, Rob would have just headed due west after he dropped the burner handcomm in a bush. Found a place out closer to the residential districts that would be serving a greasy, heavy breakfast this morning. Taken some time to misdirect everyone some more while he found a safe way home.

But this might be his only chance to prove something to himself.

He had no idea who might be coming to pick him up, so they would expect him to just be hanging around out front somewhere watching. Or worse, sitting inside with a coffee and a donut in front of him while he frantically watched people coming in and cars driving through the lot.

If this was all just a group of ex-boyfriends with military training and equipment, that was one thing. But they'd been hunting him hard enough that at least twice someone had managed to hit stone or trees within five meters of a desperately-fleeing Handsome Rob.

Ex-boyfriends weren't supposed to be that good.

So he'd laid his own trap. Dropped the phone, once he

was sure Dolf had had time to track it. Set off the special timer that would cause the innards to melt themselves into a puddle in two minutes, so nobody could figure out what that crazy redneck Nigel had done to it after purchase.

Rob wouldn't be in that donut shop. *Low trust.* That place was a deathtrap with his name on it.

Instead, he moved west three blocks and then began to loop carefully around. He couldn't act suspicious as he walked, on the assumption that someone might see something.

The wrong kind of someone. The kind of someone who might land their vehicle hard on the pavement as a group of well-armed ex-boyfriends suddenly bailed out and opened fire.

At least there were more people at this time. Puerto Peñasco never really slept, but it was a government town for the most part, and folks did weekend at least as well here as they did in Lincoln. Runners were out now, grinding their solitary klicks with the headphones in. Donut shops were pulling the good ones out of the oil and sprinkling them with powdered sugar or glaze. Coffee shops would be turning on the "Caffeine Warning" lights soon.

The city would be waking up.

The sky was hazy and overcast. It had rained at one point while he'd slept, evidenced by the occasional puddles now, but nothing like fog. Cool enough that his jacket was good, but he didn't need anything heavier, unless he was going to sleep rough.

He had two spare identities in Nigel's kits that he could activate if he had to. Adequate to sleep nice and order room service, if he was still running loose in twelve hours.

Worry about that if it came.

No, he needed to see who was watching.

Rob didn't believe for an instant that he'd be alone with

whoever drove up. Nobody had that big a deathwish, so Dolf would quietly send help along. Probably on the ground. If they went high enough to not be seen, they'd be in those low clouds, and Rob had originally been hired because nothing about him stood out physically from a distance.

Nothing memorable on a scanner, except what the Service had taught him. And what Jorge had improved on.

Rob had been a Courier when he first joined the Service. His very first mission as a Field Agent had paired him with the *Can't Shoot Straight Gang* to pull off the most audacious Grand Theft Starship anybody could remember.

A year later, the *Can't Shoot Straight Gang* had returned, and again done the impossible. Maybe not as perfectly invisible as the first job, but Jorge had stayed in touch with some of those Corynthe pirates and shot a lot of secondary footage with Rodderick Kedzierski on the way home from *6725 Lacertae.*

Hell, Jorge had even decided to get the funding he needed to make a movie from all the bits and pieces that he and Roxy had assembled in the process of capturing and destroying that pirate base.

Those damned pirates from *Salonnia* couldn't have found him that fast, could they?

No, it must be someone else, assuming his own paranoia hadn't gotten the better of him. Espionage was a job that called for your crazier instincts to be honed and listened to, not ignored.

So assume a panel van of some sort. There were a bunch of those on the streets making deliveries right now, competing with the flatbeds bringing in fresh vegetables from the greenhouses on the outskirts of town. Plus fishermen heading down to the marina for a run, having probably either opened some restaurant, or having come from their favorite all-night joint.

That meant the bad guys couldn't be too close, if they really existed and wanted to be waiting for him. Nobody would want to get caught up in a firefight in the parking lot of a donut shop on a Saturday morning. If nothing else, your reputation as a pro would never recover.

No, they'll be out some distance. Sniper, instead of a walk-up.

Long shot from someplace with enough elevation that a truck on the road at the wrong moment wouldn't ruin everything and let your prey escape.

Weren't many of those sorts of places in that area. Which was exactly why Rob had chosen it.

He slipped into a loading dock area in an alley off Ninth, four blocks over, and pulled another of Nigel's toys out. There was a fire door down here, so he put the device against the lock mechanism and pushed the button, putting it to work.

An employee would have the right fob, probably built into a small ID placard hung around their neck, or maybe from their belt. It would get close and the machine would issue a challenge ping.

Commercial model like this only had two hundred and fifty-five possible combinations. This was to keep amateurs out, not protect the crown jewels.

The door clicked and Rob pulled it open, grabbing his nifty toy and slipping inside. Up a nearby flight of stairs, following a path Jorge and he had carved out for exactly this sort of never-going-to-happen emergency that was happening today.

Observation deck with plants on the fourteenth floor. No outside access, so no chance of interrupting anybody doing naughty things, unless it ended up being a pair of accountants having a really kinky affair. Rob wasn't about to judge, all things considered. Goose and gander, as it were.

Out of the big bag, he pulled a tripod and a pair of electronic opera glasses, looking almost like a surveyor's transom and lenses. He hadn't asked Nigel where the parts came from.

Quick scan. Rotate. Up. Across. There.

Ah, crap.

Rob blew out an angry breath and clenched his fists so he didn't punch anything. Locked the transom in and dialed the image down tight rather like a kind of sniper rifle they called an Iron Monster. The kind you used when you had a non-moving target at extreme ranges, where even humidity had to be factored into your shot.

Rob hadn't made it to the next rank in the Service yet, but that was most likely coming, once he finished some more training and schooling.

When they promoted him to Assassin.

Having something long and heavy and explosive right now might improve his humor, as he watched a team of four men set up, two blocks over and on a rooftop Jorge had identified as a good place to shoot from if this sort of situation ever came up.

One shooter with a bipod and a big, glass scope on a rifle. One spotter next to him with glass binoculars rather than electronics. Two others on the rear flanks, out of the way, but standing nonchalantly with pistols.

None of the faces were men he knew, which he at least found somewhat reassuring. He'd been right about everything feeling like a trap from the moment someone's foot impacted on his door two hours before.

Now he had proof.

Whatever was going on, it wasn't the whole Service out to do him wrong. A rogue of some sort, for reasons Rob could only guess at. But at the very least someone inside the Service had told them where to find him. Someone who knew Handsome Rob Segura would be standing at the corner of Ninth and Academy in a few minutes, politely waiting for someone to rudely put a bullet in him.

Rob snapped pictures of the men. They'd be a little fuzzy at this range, but not so bad that the human eye wouldn't be able to identify the shooters later, and a little magic down in the Data Analysis Inspectorate would probably clean them up enough to find matching records in criminal databanks.

He doubted these men officially existed. That was the easiest way to disappear. At the same time, he would be able to alert his bosses that they did have a leak.

A mole.

An insider, doing naughty things against someone that many might consider the Golden Boy right now.

Rob growled, but quietly, not wanting to disturb anyone if they had decided to go at it in the bushes around this sun room.

He collapsed the opera glasses and tripod. Slipped them back into his bag, and considered his next step.

Someone had decided to hunt Handsome Rob.

Time to return the favor.

10

"Anything?" Dodger asked from his spot at the rear, guarding the stairwell door they'd used to get up here, in case someone just happened to come up here to watch the sun rise, or something equally ludicrous.

"Negative," Lan replied, never taking his eye from the binoculars as he slowly panned around the parking lot.

Kovalchuk was dialed in on the door of the shop with the big rifle, waiting for a target assignment.

Dodger checked his watch again. Five minutes early and waiting, but nobody had gone into or out of the shop that was even close to the description of the target.

He wondered briefly if the man had given them the slip, but he could just as easily be watching from a nearby alleyway. Kovalchuk's rifle would penetrate anything short of an armored car at this range, so it wasn't like the target could get away, especially not when a secondary bursting charge detonated. If it was inside the car, everything would be hit. If the shot just hit the target and passed through, presumably the explosion would be in the pavement close by.

Either way, the team would have to vanish quickly,

because someone would be able to vector cops this way. Those sorts of things happened when wars broke out in the middle of otherwise peaceful cities.

"Think I got the car," Lan said suddenly. "Gray sedan at the light, second in line."

"Stay with it," Dodger said.

Just because the morning had gone that far sideways, he looked up, making sure there weren't any drones or low-flying vehicles overhead that might be able to spot them and be able to identify anyone later. Kovalchuk could probably bring down anything if he had to, but Dodger would be much happier just hopping in an elevator when this was done and having Swede drive them sedately away.

"Car just came to the driveway," Lan said. "Turning in now. Found himself a parking spot. You'll have a shot at the target's back as he opens the door."

"Got it," Kovalchuk grunted. "Locked on the passenger door. Somebody find me the rabbit."

"Looking," Lan replied. "Nobody moving out of pattern."

Pattern.

Every city, every neighborhood had a pattern. A flow. Dodger and his team would stand out against this sort of place, if anyone saw them right now. That would lead to memories later.

Troublesome memories, perhaps.

Their target today wasn't supposed to be that good.

"What's he doing?" Dodger asked quietly.

"Car's parked," Kovalchuk said.

"Other folks are walk-up, but they've all gone into the store," Lan said. "Nobody remotely similar to our target. I got old geezers out for a morning cinnamon roll. Crazy jogger ladies in skintight outfits. Nobody male under sixty."

"Keep looking," Dodger said.

He had a bad feeling about this. Decades in the industry of death and destruction usually gave you a sixth sense for this sort of trouble. He'd ignored it last night when the voice told him to just blow the whole damned apartment to hell with high explosives instead of knocking.

But their principal had wanted an assassination, not a terrorist incident. Wrong sort of message being sent.

That voice was muttering right now that they'd been made. That the target had smelled something earlier and sent everybody on a wild goose chase while he was off having breakfast and probably laughing to himself about all the grief he was causing them.

You'll get yours, boy.

But he had to remain outwardly calm. Almost bored. The command decurion keeping everyone on the straight and narrow here. Just another job. Just another day at the office.

He didn't believe it, but if he wished hard enough, maybe the target would have a stupid fit and walk into the parking lot right now, pausing to look around so Kovalchuk could drill him.

Seconds turned into minutes.

"Anything?"

Kovalchuk was getting anxious now. Never a good sign. Your shooter needed to be utter calmness, but he was effectively blind with the need to keep his shot lined up.

"Nothing," Lan said, also wound a little tighter than he should be.

They could smell it, too. The target had bailed on the meet.

It happened to everyone.

With pros, it was even relatively common, as cold feet would cause someone to fall back on secondary and tertiary options, rather than take any chance.

His men were also pros, though. They stayed on target.

Dodger turned to Arni, quiet in his corner watching north on Academy.

Arni shook his head. Nothing up this way.

Nothing.

"I have movement," Lan called, drawing everyone back down to focus. "Driver just opened his door and got out. Not looking around at all. Walking inside."

Yes, that made sense. Maybe the target was dumb enough to be hiding inside, trapped. The driver could make contact. Or the target might pass him a message.

Something. Anything.

They had no vision into the shop from here, in spite of all the glass around the place. Unless someone was stupid enough to sit by a window. Or suicidal enough, but the target had moved like a man who wanted to outlive them all by decades.

"Still nothing off pattern," Lan said a moment later.

Dodger already knew that the meet was scrubbed, but they had to wait here, waiting for the triple cross on the part of the target. Maybe he'd race out at the last moment, just as the driver was about to leave. Or maybe even wait until the car was backed around and about to hit the street.

Maybe the target was in a side street watching right now, expecting the ambush at the donut shop, and would step out once the car was back on the street.

Dodger felt like he was in somebody's crosshairs now. Waiting for them to take a shot he would never hear, only feel when it impacted on his body armor plates and penetrated.

More time passed uncomfortably.

If it was his mission, Dodger would have already scrubbed and run, expecting that someone had called the police and that heavy teams were quietly racing to surround this building and take them alive or dead.

He wasn't calling the shots here, so he couldn't just call someone and say they would need to try again later. The principal would be expecting their to give their professional all on this.

Waiting to the very end, however painfully that might come about.

The driver emerged.

"Movement," Lan yelled. "Looks like the driver."

"Do I take him down?" Kovalchuk asked.

Another option was the shell game. Send one man in, swap jackets, and the target walks out, driving away while you look for someone to get into the passenger seat.

"Negative," Lan said. "Same man as went in. They should have picked someone who looked more like the target if that was the game. Short, broad, and blond won't cut it."

Dodger nodded to himself. It was a shitshow, but nobody would be able to accuse his team of half-assing it.

"Driver got himself breakfast," Lan announced. "Maybe a message was passed, but I do not have another target."

"Stay with them until the vehicle is out of sight," Dodger said. "I'm guessing we're scrubbed, but we'll get asked later."

"Roger that," Lan replied. "Driver is in the vehicle now. Buckling his seat belt. Starting things up and adjusting his radio. Probably reporting to his bosses. In gear and backing, stay awake for breaks. Nothing. Stopped. Forward. At the street, stopped for traffic. Expect a runner. Nothing. Nothing. Break in traffic coming. Movement. Turning. Nothing. And out of sight from here."

"Pack it up tight," Dodger said. "Stay loose and expect that we'll get a call shortly, so catnap in the car for now. We won't go off duty until we get told to."

He slipped the door to the stairwell open and pointed his pistol at the empty semi-darkness.

Somehow, he had been unconsciously expecting his

target to be standing there with a pulse carbine, but he was alone.

Behind him. Dodger heard the others stashing gear in bags and moving with professional speed.

He would need to call this one in, but not until they were in the car and moving.

Harder for a target to track them that way.

Whoever that son of a bitch was.

11

———

A KNOCK AT THE DOOR CAUSED MIGUEL TO LOOK UP. Most of this building was startlingly primitive, compared to what was possible with a culture that spanned planetary systems. But it was too easy to compromise electronic communications, so many things were manual, or hard-wired if necessary. A hand knocking on a wooden door, rather than a computerized system that any competent redneck could abuse.

Miguel was familiar with at least one of those.

Still, he was in his office, at the very heart of the system that was the *Lincolnshire Guardia Civil Interior*. The Service itself was run from here on the sixth floor.

Miguel closed the paper file he had been reading and slid it anonymously into a pile on his left.

"Come," he called loud enough to be heard through the stout, wooden panel.

Stansfield Brightmeadow-Gates opened the door rather like an undertaker with a tape measure in one hand and stepped just across the threshold. The look on his face suggested that the news would not be pleasant.

Miguel waited patiently.

"Alcazar has passed along a message, sir," the man said eloquently. "The meeting did not occur as planned. Segura was a no-show."

"And the other comm unit?" Miguel went ahead and asked anyway.

"Searchers apparently discovered it abandoned in Hidalgo Park," the man continued. "Initial reports suggest it was inoperable. The device is being investigated off-site before it is brought here, against potential risk."

"Very good," Miguel said. "Let Dolf know that I'd like a briefing sometime just after lunch, assuming that's possible, just to keep me in the loop for when I need to communicate with the Minister. She'll be at her weekend place, so I may need to fly up there around dinner, if this hasn't all been settled."

"Understood," Stansfield said dryly, closing the door in his wake and leaving Miguel alone with his stacks of paper in various files.

The business of espionage never slept, so he already frequently worked six days in the office, but he would make it up to himself and Caroline with a long weekend soon. A phone ringing in the pre-dawn hours almost always meant that he'd be in the office instead of whatever he had planned.

Miguel pulled the personnel file that he had been reading back out from the pile and reviewed it. Nothing about Roberto Segura stood out as new or obvious, even though the file had been up to date as recently as perhaps Wednesday.

They would need to list a new address for him soon. Assuming that he made it someplace safe.

Jorge Royo and his veteran team had accepted the man as an assistant when Miguel had first cleared him as a Field Agent. Everything since then just lent credence to what a good idea that had been. The usual foibles and affairs of a young man vibrantly alive and working in the more dangerous parts of the industry, as compared to the generally dry and bland folks who came out of Data Analysis, like Stansfield Brightmeadow-Gates.

Miguel keyed the intercom to his personal assistant, Ben.

"Yes, Director?" Ben came on the line immediately.

Thinking about his assistant, Miguel always found it terribly instructive how young the Service was. Ben was only thirty-one years old, and already near the top of where he could be promoted, unless he took a lateral and ended up in one of the Inspectorates.

But espionage was a young person's field. All of Miguel's Inspectorates were run right now by folks just on either side of fifty, and even he was only fifty-four. Only Stansfield Brightmeadow-Gates really stood out, but he was perhaps the last of the previous generation in the Service still active. They used to say that the building was erected around that man.

"Send a note down to Esmeralda in Data Analysis, Ben," Miguel ordered. "I want to hear about any incidents of force or violence that get police calls, as soon as Dolf does. In fact, have her come up here now so I can ask her a few questions directly."

"Understood, Director," Ben said.

Miguel released the hard-wired line and contemplated things.

He wasn't terribly surprised that Segura had missed the meeting. A good agent would intentionally keep walking if they smelled a trap.

Miguel was certain that the dead handcomm had been modified at some point by Phipps. Now that it had been slagged, they didn't have a direct method of contacting Segura. At least, assuming that Segura's personal handcomm, the Service-issued one, had been destroyed or lost in the madcap mayhem of the early morning that had started the day.

A few minutes later, Esmeralda MacTavish was admitted to his sanctum.

She could have been one of the *Cowboys on Three* in her time, had she wanted. At a vibrant fifty-one, she was still graceful, tall, and beautiful enough to turn heads anywhere that she went. Dark blond hair only now starting to stripe. Had once been married, but the fool had decided to have an affair with his driver and she'd been single for the last two decades. No scandals inside the building or publicly, so if she had dated, she'd maintained a very private tone to things.

She was still one his favorites, brilliant as well as competent. Had she not been such an amazing nerd, she might have been pushed out of the nest of Data Analysis twenty years ago, but they had lots of cowboys they could recruit.

Very few mathematicians ever made the grade around here.

"Good morning, Miguel," she said as he sat her in the one chair on that side of the large desk he kept between himself and visitors. "I presume I got called in at the same time you did, but Dolf won't share much with me."

"Not sure there's much to tell, Esme," Miguel smiled. Of all his direct reports, she might be the only one he classified as a friend, rather than merely a co-worker of long duration. "An incident has been unfolding, but we are very much in the dark here, at least for now."

"So I gather," she smiled. "What was it that required you to send poor Ben scrambling frantically down to my office to bring me here?"

"The call you routed to the War Room earlier came from what I believe they call a burner handcomm," Miguel noted.

"That's right," Esmeralda nodded. "Dolf challenged the man directly, and got the right response."

"Do we know what happened to Segura's regular device?" Miguel asked.

He rather liked the smile that emerged.

"Dolf's folks went and retrieved it, once I had told them where to look," Esmeralda said tartly. "Segura had apparently placed an unanswered call to Mrs. Jones and then tossed it into the back of a moving vegetable truck, presumably as he emerged from his hiding place. We backtracked, but the vehicle did not go directly past Segura's building."

"Did anyone show up looking for the device before Dolf's team got there?" Miguel asked in a tight careful voice.

"What are you suggesting, Miguel?" She caught his tension and leaned forward to stare at him.

"Segura missed the arranged meeting a few minutes ago," he replied. "Considering that his home address should not be known at all, I'm pursuing a thread that perhaps some portion of our communications infrastructure has been compromised."

"Are you accusing me?" her voice turned tart.

"If you've gone rogue, Esme, the service is so entirely compromised that they might as well burn the building down, salt the earth, and hire folks over into the Office of Naval Intelligence to replace us."

She smiled at that. It was a running joke these days how incompetent *ONI* was generally seen to be by professional organizations. Far too often, the Service had been called in when the navy had failed.

"So what are you suggesting then?" she asked.

"If someone else showed up, looking for Segura's handset, then things were already compromised," Miguel said.

"And you don't trust Dolf's teams to investigate?"

"I barely trust myself, Esme," Miguel countered. "I'd like

you to make some quiet calls outside, to some friends you can trust to keep their mouths shut. Ask them to poke around. I don't particularly care who it was, if anything happened. Just the fact itself is good enough for me. At that point, you'll need to figure out how to step outside your own organization so we can reach Segura and get him home safely."

"Because someone on the inside is leaking," she noted.

"I have had my suspicions, ere now, Esmeralda," Miguel turned serious. "Nothing that even casts a shadow. More a scent in the air."

"Is your office safe?" she asked, looking around.

"Again, your folks are responsible," Miguel said. "If this space is violated, then the list of people who could do it is so amazingly short that we'll end up having to go to the Governor of *Ramsey* himself. And probably retire to our pensions, those of us who aren't in prison."

"Understood, Miguel," she said. "I think you're starting at shadows, but I'll see what light I can bring to it. You'll be in all day?"

"At least until I need to catch a flight up to brief the Minister at her weekend place," he replied. "Verbal briefing only."

"Brightmeadow-Gates?" she inquired.

"He has enough to keep him busy for now," Miguel decided. "Let's just keep this between us. Perhaps we can have lunch down in the canteen later."

"If someone could pry you out of this office," she smiled as she rose.

Miguel felt better as she made her way out and closed the door behind her.

Something smelled rotten.

The only question was how high the rot had reached.

12

Rob had always found it useful to have friends outside the usual circles. A Field Agent was supposed to cultivate all manner of contacts to make their lives easier on planets where they traveled regularly, but he didn't stop there. Normally, it also meant bartenders and folks working at restaurants, but in Rob's case, he'd followed Jorge's instructions to maintain almost a double life here in Puerto Peñasco.

Once he had spotted the shooting team, the hardest part had been sneaking by his own folks, without knowing where they were hiding, to get to the building with the snipers.

At least those men were professionals. Getaway car stashed in an alley, ready to drop out onto Tenth when trouble erupted a few blocks away. Driver hunched down and mostly hidden from outside view, but that just meant that he couldn't look in the mirror when Rob stuck his head and his camera around the corner long enough to snap pictures of the plates and disappear.

It didn't help that Rob was a fugitive right now, but the

man he wanted to call owed him big time. Especially for that one redhead Rob had introduced him to.

He pulled out a second burner from the bag and dialed a number from memory. At least the sun was close enough to rising, and the guy was used to getting strange calls. Police detectives never led normal lives.

Two rings and a profanity as Police Detective Ahmed McIntyre al-Inverness answered. About what Rob had been expecting, calling this early.

"It's Handsome Rob," he replied simply, checking around as he walked, but nobody seemed to be paying attention.

"You got any idea what time it is?" Ahmed snarled.

"I need a favor," Rob cut the man off. "Quietly. Maybe dangerously. Shit's gone sideways."

That got through to the man.

"Talk to me," Ahmed said.

From the sound, the cop was already out of bed and probably pulling on pants right now, gun resting on a dresser nearby within easy reach. Badge next to that.

"Since you were asleep, someone else got the call," Rob said. "Someone tried to kick in my door a few hours ago. When I got away, they blew the place up."

"How the hell did they find you?" Ahmed asked. "I don't even know where you live."

"That's the problem, Ahmed," Rob replied. "I don't exist. Someone told them where to look."

"These folks got a name?" Ahmed asked.

"Got a license number," Rob said. "Didn't recognize any of them, but they were pros. Heavily armed. And following me places they shouldn't be able to."

"Who are you, Handsome Rob?" Ahmed asked. "Seriously."

"Ahmed, I'm a spy," Rob told him. "A Field Agent for the *Lincolnshire Guardia Civil Interior.*"

"No shit?"

"No shit," Rob said.

Just because, he ducked into a doorway of a closed bookshop, pivoted and looked for anyone breaking pattern behind him. Only the dog across the street and back a half-block seemed to be paying any attention.

"Why aren't you calling your people?" Ahmed asked.

"They were the only ones who knew where to find me the second time, al-Inverness," Rob said. "Nobody high on my trust list right now, but at the same time, not many people should connect me with you. I certainly don't trust the police to keep their mouths shut, even if they were to take me into protective custody. That just lines me up for an assassin."

"Give me the license number," Ahmed decided. "You be at this number?"

"Yes, but I'm turning the device off and pulling the battery as soon as we're done talking, just in case," Rob said, feeding the cop the license number of that sedan. "Don't do anything official if you find them. I'll call you in an hour or two, once I get someplace safe."

He powered the device down, broke it back into pieces, and slid them back into their various pouches.

If the shooters were locals, then he'd drop the cops on them, just to be a shit. Out of towners would have a rental that could be traced, hopefully. Maybe the vehicle was just stolen, but that would mean that any cop could pull them over, so Rob doubted they'd go down that path.

Too amateur.

He still wasn't sure who he could trust at headquarters.

Maybe he'd just have to take these pigs down by himself.

Or with a few friends.

13

———

ROB WASN'T USUALLY UP EARLY ENOUGH TO HIT THIS
place for breakfast. And brunch was best done somewhere
else, most days when he was off-duty and in town.

Only the luck of the gods that he'd felt like staying in last
night, watching a movie, and going to bed at a reasonable
hour. Otherwise, he might have been coming home about
the time the ex-boyfriends decided to rumble the place.

That would have left one Field Agent splattered on a side
street, more likely than not, so he wasn't going to look this
gift horse in the mouth. He already should have probably
been dead a few times in the last four hours.

Rob slid into a small booth clear at the back, out of sight
of the front door until you were inside and past the gruff
woman protecting the place.

Wasn't too crowded yet, as Puerto Peñasco didn't get up
that early on the weekends, and he was too far from the
marinas to compete with fishermen already out on the water
today.

Coffee. Utterly necessary at this point. Adulterated with
honey and milk for the extra fat and energy as a layer on top

of the caffeine. He had his messenger bag handy, making him look like an *artisté*, missing only the beret.

If your art was armed mayhem, maybe.

Jorge, Roxy, and Nigel were off planet for a few more days at a minimum, so someone had known when to hit. Longbow was locked in an old monastery recording feverishly, last Rob had heard. Hopefully, he and his band were safe, and whoever it was had wanted to make this personal.

Rob kept circling back to the snipers on the roof. He'd arranged the meeting with Dolf, but that included anyone in the room at that moment, plus whoever else was in that loop. Probably twenty or thirty names, if Dolf had had no reason to tighten things down at that point.

Hopefully, Dolf wasn't the one who had set him up. Rob would feel pretty stupid later, arranging with his own boss for the man to assassinate him.

Who did that leave to trust?

Nobody. At least no insiders.

And even if Rob had had a vehicle, trying to trail five armed killers by himself was a quick way to get himself killed. He was better off letting everyone get away and resetting the board. At least for now.

At some point, maybe Ahmed would come through with an address, and he could work on his own ambush. Rob had friends in this town, although he supposed Ahmed would want in on it, and a cop wouldn't necessarily play nice with the sorts of criminals and smugglers who owed Rob favors.

Recruit his own gang of cops for this? Bigger and dumber than some ideas, but probably easier to keep it quiet later, since those sorts of folks could be ordered to stay silent under pain of an official sanction that mean nobody would hire them beyond a corner bodega.

"What'll it be?" the waiter circled around and smiled at Rob.

Rob considered how likely it was that he wouldn't get a chance to eat again today.

"The SOS Plate," he decided. "With cheese on top of the gravy."

"How do you want your steak?"

"Medium rare," Rob said. "Eggs over easy. Potatoes extra crispy."

"Coming up."

Yeah, a heavy breakfast was called for. He could always grab a burrito from a bodega later, if he was idling.

All he had to do was disappear for a while, until certain folks got complacent, and others began to panic.

Someone needed to learn the lesson that hunting Handsome Rob was a stupid idea.

14

Dodger had waited until they were driving away before he triggered the signal that he needed to check in. Ops rules said he never called the principal, so had pushed a little button that turned on a little light on the handcomm and waited.

The unit buzzed almost immediately.

"Status?" the scrambled voice asked.

"Target was a no-show," Dodger said simply. "The pickup vehicle arrived, the driver went inside, but the target did not emerge. If they met later, we were not in a position to observe."

"Your target apparently aborted," the voice said. "Were you seen?"

"Anything is possible, but we are still at large, awaiting orders."

"Stand down for now," the principal said. "The target will need to make contact again to arrange extraction. At that point, I will be in touch."

He hung up without waiting for a response, so Dodger slipped the handcomm back into his pocket and grimaced.

"Destination?" Swede asked from the driver's seat.

"None," Dodger said. "Target has vanished. This may be a full scrub."

"Food, then?" Lan asked.

"Yeah," Dodger decided. "We're supposed to stand down and sit on our thumbs until we hear back, so let's head down to the marina and eat there. Should be quiet enough at this time of day, since the pretty boys and girls won't be out for a while."

And it would keep them relatively close to the center of things, without being too close. Right on an edge where they could swoop in quickly if they needed to.

Dodger's only fear now was that the target would steal a car or ride a bus all the way to the edge of town and make it to a safe house nobody had told Dodger about.

They could hit such a place, but those were normally supposed to be as reinforced as the target's apartment had proven.

Of course, after all this effort and annoyance, maybe they'd blast the place first. They could sift the ashes for evidence afterwards.

Or not.

15

—————

MIGUEL NODDED TO BEN AND THE MAN WITHDREW, admitting Esmeralda to the inner sanctum of Miguel's office.

She paused to close the door, pull a device from a pocket of her long jacket, and thumb a button. Jammer/scanner. Locate all the transmitters, then play a sound to pick up ones only voice activated.

Miguel felt the temperature of the room drop a few degrees as she walked closer and then sat without a word.

"That bad?" he asked in a quiet voice, aware that some recorders might only burst transmit later, when nobody was paying attention.

"That paranoid, perhaps," Esmeralda replied just as quietly. "Nobody called the police this morning, but a small group of men appeared on that loading dock armed. They looked around quickly and then left almost immediately, but it was obvious that they were looking for Segura's handcomm. Tracking on the frequency, which they would only know if someone told them how to do it."

"A mole," Miguel nodded, understanding.

A worm inside the apple, slowly boring their way along, with all the rot invisible beneath a shiny exterior.

Assassinating Rob Segura wouldn't have necessarily revealed them, had it worked out the way it had probably been planned. It was only when things went wrong that unexpected edges appeared. Miguel wondered what other *accidents* might not have been.

"Now what?" she asked in a grim, unforgiving voice, probably presuming that the traitor was inside her Inspectorate.

Miguel had his doubts on that point.

"Normally, I would task you with doing a hard audit on all Service communications over the last three days, but you probably wouldn't find anything, and mostly likely would spook our target. I'd rather capture this person than just force them from cover. Easier to explain myself to the Minister later, and protect my pension. Yours, too."

She smiled at that. Failure to capture a mole didn't mean either of them was likely to end up in jail, but it might get someone tossed out on their ass pretty quickly. Esmeralda had thirty years in at this point, while Miguel was a political appointee who had only been in the building for fifteen.

"Suggestions, then?" Esme looked at him with steel in her eyes.

"We were slack earlier, when Segura called in," Miguel said. "How many people were privy to that call?"

She leaned back and Miguel watched her eyes flicker back and forth on the wall high behind him.

"Probably twenty," she replied after a moment. "With a dozen more in the loop after that. One of them?"

"Possibly," Miguel said. "Possibly not. But perhaps Segura presumed that his communications were compromised enough at the beginning to trigger the device and cause it to send someone awry. And then he missed the meeting later. We have no witnesses, but I suspect that the same people who followed his handcomm onto a loading dock with guns were somehow hidden nearby when he was supposed to make contact, and he saw them."

"Is Segura really that good?" Esmeralda asked, possibly irked by the whole thing, but like Brightmeadow-Gates, the folks in Data Analysis believed that patiently building up a portfolio of pieces, rather like one made a pearl, was the best way to do things.

The system still failed often enough, however, that you needed folks like Royo and Segura involved.

"He has scored well enough on various tests and exams to suggest that he has the potential, yes," Miguel said. "And my Special Operations team certainly as accepted him as one of them, so I'm willing to listen to folks who have been doing this sort of thing since before you even joined the Service, Esmeralda."

She scowled, but Miguel doubted it was personal. Everyone else had their own opinions of the *Cowboys on Three*, but it was generally just a professional rivalry thing, the left hand frequently jealous of the right hand for getting all the accolades.

"Dolf will want to be in on things at this point," she noted. "One of his boys, and rescuing him will be a field operation."

"Undoubtedly," Miguel felt his face turn into a rather feral, angry smile. "But most of the people on your list of suspects will come from Operations by the nature of things this morning, and we don't know which ones to exclude without risking Segura."

"I don't like the gleam in your eyes, Miguel," Esmeralda said sternly.

No, he supposed she wouldn't. But he wasn't the sort of

trained agent to undertake the things he had in mind, and she was.

"Now I really don't like that smile," she continued. "What are you up to?"

"Dolf will need to run things as normal," Miguel said. "As you noted, that's his job. But I don't know where the mole is, assuming at this point that we have one, so I want to use Dolf and his folks as stalking goats. They'll take charge of rescuing Segura, but you and I need to be paying attention to the shadows, to see who's up to naughty things. The best time to catch someone is with their hand literally in the cookie jar."

"And how do we do that?"

"At some point, Segura will contact us again," Miguel said. "That is my fervent hope, at least. The call will come in to one of your folks, who will route it up to Dolf immediately for confirmation. I propose cutting the Gordian knot in twain at that point."

"How, exactly?" she nearly sneered at him, but that was also to be expected.

"Assuming everything else, route the wrong information about the meeting to everyone outside Dolf's immediate team, and then have a spotter on hand at the new location to see if trouble shows up."

"And because you don't trust anyone right now…?"

"You and I will handle that part ourselves," he said. "I'm happy to be bait, if need be, and you can be the competent field agent you used to be, back when we were young."

"That's completely insane, Miguel," she said.

"Perhaps," he agreed. "But do you know a better way to distract everyone?"

"Several, in fact," she retorted sharply. "It would be simple enough to fabricate a message from Segura and leak it internally, if you want everyone distracted. I have absolutely no business being in the field, and you have even less."

"Quite possibly," Miguel said. "But if we do have a traitor inside this building right now, the only way to save the Service itself is to catch them ourselves. Otherwise, the Minister will probably have to purge the organization and rebuild from scratch with a new generation of agents. I'd rather not."

She fell silent for a moment, face composed and about as angry as he could ever remember seeing her.

"Suppose we could contact Segura, when he does check in," she said after a moment. "Send him a secret message. Would you remain here if you could use the man as your hunter?"

"How would you do that?" Miguel asked. "And yes, to your latter question. As I said earlier, if you've gone rogue, we're all out of work and possibly in prison in a month, Esmeralda."

She smiled at that.

"So if you're serious, Miguel, then you stay here," she said. "Watch my back while I go out and rescue your young man."

"Our young man," Miguel corrected her.

"Who has a reputation as a ladies man, Miguel," she snapped. "Another one of Jorge Royo's disciples who has decided that emulating that old goat is the best way to be successful."

"It has served him well, I might point out," Miguel tried to placate her. "Royo speaks well of Rob."

"Well, hopefully he's smart enough to keep his wits about him and his hands to himself, if I'm out there attempting to rescue him," she said flatly. "The last thing I need is some punk fool getting it into his mind to try to seduce me, as if I was some target on one of his missions."

"I believe Segura is brighter than that," Miguel said. "Our Mrs. Jones speaks well of him also and she has far less tolerance for most things."

"Miguel, I'm twice his age," she sneered.

"And single, gorgeous, brilliant, and competent," he retorted with a grin at her and a droll tone. "I can't see how *any* man or most women would find that particular combination attractive. Besides, I suspect he's much more interested in coming in from the cold than having you warm his bed. At least in the present tense. What you two might do in your off hours only becomes my problem if it becomes a threat to the Service."

"Seriously, Miguel?" she asked tartly.

"Yes, seriously, Esme," he said. "You figure out how to contact him. How to get him to safety, even if it's off-planet until we can bring in some people who are not possibly involved in the current issues. I will cover for you here, and leave secret instructions with the Minister, in case something happens to me."

"And what happens here?" she asked. "What will you be doing?"

"Nothing for the time being," Miguel decided. "Knowing that we are to some level compromised, we allow the situation to remain calm enough that it is no longer a ticking bomb scenario. You and yours will have to do some of the work tracking, since we need to assume that the communications about Segura are originating inside this building. They will leave footprints in the snow that can be tracked."

Esmeralda studied him for a long, angry second, as if she was about to storm out of his office, slam the door behind her, and write a letter to the Minister. She'd probably remain within bounds when she did, and he'd end up having a long, delicate conversation with a small group of elected officials who would react like headless chickens, but the alternatives involved Star Chambers, secret governmental investigations that didn't have to follow any sort of laws, because everyone involved had already signed away their rights at some a point.

He would do anything to avoid bringing that level of suspicion to the Service. Those investigators would bring a sledgehammer to the problem, rather than a scalpel, and the damage to *Lincolnshire's* intelligence apparatus would be incalculable.

Then she smiled.

It was literally a breathtaking event when she did that. Had he not known better, Miguel would have believed the woman was thirty-one, rather than fifty-one when she smiled. Any color on her hair for the graying stripes and she could give many lies that nobody would be able to penetrate.

"You're going to owe me for this, Miguel," Esmeralda MacTavish said with a grin.

"If you've saved the Service from destruction, I will pretty much owe you everything, Esme," he grinned back. "Try not to bleed me completely dry on the next budgetary cycle?"

"No promises," Esme said as she rose, more relaxed now. "My file has a series of challenge codes in it for compromised communications. I will talk with one of my folks that I trust, and have her handle Segura's next call, while I take the rest of the weekend off, returning to the plans I had originally made, at least as far as the rest of this building is concerned. I will call you on your personal line once I know something, or send messages. Hopefully, it will all work out and this will be just a training exercise to prove I have been keeping my skills sharp."

"Thank you, Esmeralda," Miguel said seriously. "I'm not talking to anyone but you at this point, until we determine how bad things have gotten."

He rose and took her hand, a personal conspiracy that would see them through, or take them all down.

As she exited, Miguel considered sending Ben down to retrieve her file, but decided that he should do it himself. Not even Ben or Stansfield needed to be looped in on this.

Miguel had never run an agent in the field, but he understood the techniques and methods, having debriefed enough agents and read enough reports.

But if it had gotten to this point, should he perhaps consider retiring when this situation was resolved and leaving a clean slate for whoever came after him? Clean up the mess and walk away?

How bad had he let things get on his watch?

16

____

Rob took a deep breath as he exited the
restaurant, stuffed beyond full right now and so overly-
caffeinated that he was almost surprised he wasn't hovering
just above the ground.

There might be something to getting up early and having
that amazing a breakfast to start the day. Not every day, mind
you, because staying out dancing was still more fun, but he'd
be thirty soon, and theoretically slowing down as he
matured.

If Jorge's pattern for living could be classified as mature.

The restaurant had been on the ground floor of a mixed-
use building, right at the edge of where the towers started to
give way to single-family home neighborhoods, as you moved
up the socio-economic ladder and wanted your kids to have a
yard and a dog.

Handsome Rob didn't see that in his future. The Service
was so much better, and he couldn't see a spouse putting up
with the extended separations his life entailed. Unless he
found an artist who might not even notice he was gone for a
month.

The sun was finally clear of the horizon now, lighting the streets enough that the streetlights were off and folks were starting to come out for milk and paper on their front porch, a quaintness Rob found comforting.

Other groups had begun the morning pilgrimage to the coffee and donut shops, getting what was left over after the really early birds had picked the place clean.

If he was careful, Rob could just vanish into those crowds, as long as he headed closer to town and away from the residential districts. Weekenders would protect him from observation.

At the same time, they would also hide the ex-boyfriends, if someone spotted him.

Rob slipped into a bodega at the corner of a tower and walked up to the counter with an innocent, slightly-befuddled look on his face.

"Morning," the middle-aged man behind the counter smiled. "What can I do for you?"

"Just landed last night and never made arrangements to link my handcomm to the local network," Rob lied easily, affecting an Aquitaine accent as an out-of-towner who didn't apparently have the right crystals. Or was too cheap to pay the local connection fees. "Need to get a handcomm that will last for a week while I'm here."

The man nodded knowingly. *Ramsey* was a cosmopolitan planet, in many places. Lincoln more than Puerto Peñasco generally, but the naval bases and universities around here meant that there were always tourists and visitors.

"This way," the man gestured Rob around to the back of the store, turning himself in place.

The bodega was still empty this early, but a space port meant that people might be on any personal time clock, regardless of the position of the sun.

Rob walked long ways around the glass counter to where

a handful of units were available. The prices were a bit steeper than he'd have paid at the starport terminal, or a dedicated store, when one opened in a few hours, but he had the funds and the need.

He just needed to look like an absent-minded businessman in town for meetings.

These were all crap. Base models that the man probably sold to folks who lived much closer to the edge financially than a proper society should allow, but Rob wasn't here to solve the galaxy's problems. At least not until he solved his own.

Rob knew he'd probably only use this unit once, keeping his good one for talking to folks that couldn't immediately run a hard trace backwards and find him, regardless of the number of nodes he told the system to cross before connecting.

The Service, for example.

No, use once and then maybe toss in a trash can or into the bed of a moving truck.

Rob smiled at the thought of what that might have done, had some watcher somewhere not picked him up and called in help. Rob had never seen the watcher, just felt the presence.

And run like hell when trouble showed up five minutes later.

"That one," Rob said, pointing to one in the middle. The most expensive, but he was playing a cover as a businessman, so he could run it as an expense account thing, rather than scraping by.

He was dressed too well today to hide as a bum, regardless of what some women had called him when they discovered that marriage moved off the table.

"The red one?" the proprietor asked, opening the cabinet and pulling out a box underneath.

"You bet," Rob smiled a silly smile. "Red ones go faster. Scientifically proven."

The man nodded sagely and rang it up. Rob pulled Aquitaine bills from a pocket and laid them out, further muddling things.

Hey, I just landed last night, crashed, and woke up needing a handcomm. Haven't even made it to the banks yet to change my cash.

It didn't appear to be the first time the man had gone through this routine.

"There's a fifteen percent charge on currency conversion," he said briefly.

"Not my money," Rob smiled. "Just need a receipt to turn in when I get home."

"Excellent," the proprietor said.

Quickly enough, the man made change, did his esoteric magic to activate the device onto the planetary network, and Rob was back out on the sidewalk, looking both ways and heading toward a local park that would give him some level of cover from immediate observation.

Puerto Peñasco wasn't blanketed with security cameras on every block, like some of the places Rob had been, but there were enough out there. They didn't prevent crime, but did a pretty good job of solving it later, by allowing authorities to track someone forwards and backwards from some event.

Handsome Rob was just invisible enough right now that he would only be seen on the rarest of luck, if someone handed the watchers his picture and told them to find him. But with the sun up, he would begin to leave a clearer trail, both for the authorities, who would hopefully shelter him, and for the bad guys who wanted him dead.

Rob wasn't about to trust anyone until he had a big enough audience. This whole thing felt like one person with an axe to grind, hiring a small team to do him wrong, rather than all the cops or all the spies in town coming after him.

He'd have lasted about as long as a fart in a hurricane in that case.

Making the call would start a clock, so Rob assembled his other phone first, once he had some trees and brush as visual protection. He dialed.

"How bad do you want these guys?" Ahmed asked instead of saying something so prosaic as *Hello?*

"Right now, it's professional, Ahmed," Rob replied. "Not personal. I reserve the right to change my mind later."

"Understood," Ahmed said. "Got an address for you."

"The car's local?" Rob asked, a little surprised.

Whoever hired them should have brought in talent from out of town. Lincoln or Landing. Hell of a jaunt to kill a man, but less risk of being recognized.

"It is," Ahmed's voice had a smile. "Not sure how accurate the address is, because near as I can tell it's a warehouse not far from the starport, rather than a housing block."

"No, that actually makes more sense," Rob said to his friend. "If these guys normally work-off planet, they'd store gear here when they're gone. Someone just hired them for a local job."

"And you don't trust anybody with a badge but me?" Ahmed asked, maybe a little put out.

"I only trust you because I owe you money," Rob laughed. "You can't collect if I'm dead. And I can't introduce you to any more girls, either."

"Good point," Ahmed laughed. "You'll owe me big for this. So you want help on this?"

"Gotta surveille it first," Rob said. "Might ask you to grab a few friends and help me quietly return the favor of a kicked-in door later, but probably nobody's home right now, and the place will be properly sanitized."

"It's my day off, so unless you manage to get yourself killed, I'll be around," Ahmed said. "Probably would have gone to the corner for a beer, a burger, and the game this afternoon."

"I'll shut this phone down again as soon as we're done, so you go act normal for now," Rob suggested. "Bought a burner to talk to others. And will get another one later on. And probably another one before nightfall."

"You're kinda scary, pal," Ahmed said.

"Scary business, Ahmed," Rob replied. "Thanks for helping."

"Wouldn't miss it."

Rob didn't have anything pithy to say, so he cut the line and broke the comm back down. A working unit could be traced, just from the towers pinging it occasionally, but without a battery, it was just a lump of biosilicon.

Untraceable, like he was aiming to be.

Rob considered the new burner handcomm as he pulled it out. Expensive as hell for being used for exactly one comm call, but he had a receipt. If the bad guys didn't end up killing him, that would make it reimbursable. And if they did, they wouldn't be able to loot his body for that much cash.

Win/win.

He dialed the Service number and held his breath.

"Operations, how may I route your call?" a young woman came on the line, from the sound of her voice.

"Handsome Rob, calling for Dolf," he replied, already picking up his pace as he moved along an unpaved trail that cut diagonally across the park.

"Stand by," she said, playing music for him.

Handcomm lines could be traced to a tower, which gave

someone about two blocks' radius, depending. If a team moved fast, they could drop on him, but he could also evade as much as he could.

He didn't have any re-routing going, so they'd probably nail his coordinates in about ninety seconds.

"Rob?" Dolf came on the line.

"Segura, R. Two-Five-Three-Seven-One-One."

"You missed the last meet," Dolf said simply.

"It was blown," he said, crossing a small creek with a jump. "Sniper team on a nearby roof. Lucky to get out alive."

"Not ours, Rob," Dolf's voice took on a placating tone. "Where's the next meet you want to try?"

He'd need to run like hell after dropping this phone. Luckily, he wasn't that far from the underground arcade he'd used to escape the ex-boyfriends earlier and it had tunnels every which way.

"Au Shun Bakery. Eleven AM. Wear a red carnation in a button hole," Rob grinned as he said it.

"We'll be there," Dolf said with far greater authority than was honest, but Rob wasn't counting.

Rob cut the line. The handcomm beeped with an incoming message. On a line nobody should have known to use.

What the hell?

He flipped the unit over to read the text message.

"You're compromised. Run. Call me direct. Esmeralda MacTavish."

And a number.

Rob memorized it, deleted it, and, just because he felt like being a shit, dropped the handcomm into the stream next to him. It should be waterproof for the time it would take a team to get here hunting. If they were fast.

That would give both groups something to do. Maybe even run into each other and start the sort of firefight that might sort out Rob's major difficulties in life, philosophical musings and ex-girlfriends notwithstanding.

He put his head down and jogged along the edge of the stream, down in the bed where he'd be out of sight of someone crossing the park itself looking for him.

Under the street along a scenic walkway that might be a good place to get mugged on a bad Saturday night, but he had his pistol out as he got close. Anyone trying that today probably was tired of living anyway.

Apparently the gods of pedestrians were on his side, or something. He emerged safely on the other side and dropped directly into the culvert that ran down to the river on a concrete bed that wasn't too badly strewn with trash.

Anyone up doing early morning yoga in one of the towers that happened to look down right now would be left scratching their heads, but he didn't care. None of them were smart enough to immediately call the authorities on a weird jogger.

He continued several blocks, not bothering to do anything but generate distance. The riverside area he was approaching was a mix of more parks and tourist areas that would fill up with folks in a few hours.

Hopefully.

The overcast sky rather promised rain later, so maybe only the hard-core health nuts would be out. Good in some ways, bad in others.

Burn that bridge when you get there.

Because the person who sent him that message was just about the last person on this planet he would have expected to hear from.

What the hell was the head of Data Analysis doing sending him a private message, rather than routing it through Dolf?

Unless they had already figured out that they had a mole

in their communications network. But she was in charge of that network.

Bigger trap?

Rob only knew the woman at a distance. Maybe had shared thirty words with her in the last five years, if that.

Old enough to be his mother, but still utterly stunning. And more famous in the Service for her brains than her beauty.

How convoluted a triple-cross was somebody running?

There was only one way to find out.

Hopefully, Ms. MacTavish liked surprises.

17

MIGUEL'S HANDCOMM BEEPED QUIETLY WITH A MESSAGE. Wasn't from Caroline, because she had her own ringtone programmed. He pulled it from a pocket.

Talked to my sister. Taking the rest of the day off.

Esme had made contact with Segura, hopefully. Sent off the message that would spin up a second conversation, assuming that everything worked.

Miguel slipped the comm back into the pocket of his blazer as someone knocked at the door.

"Come," he called loud enough to be heard.

Ben slipped his head in.

"Dolf Alcazar to see you," his assistant said. "Urgent."

"Send him in and hold everyone else off," Miguel said.

He was already expecting the man, as Segura must have checked in. And he had asked Dolf to brief him, but after lunch. It was barely morning yet.

Dolf still looked like hell, somehow. All the rugged masculinity was drawn now. Shadowed, perhaps, by stress-induced lines.

Ops Chiefs weren't supposed to be emotionally invested

in their agents, simply because they occasionally sent them off to die, but nobody had ever broke Dolf of that habit.

"Sit," Miguel said. "I take it something has happened?"

Dolf more or less fell into the seat and took a deep breath before he spoke.

"We just heard from Segura," he began in a flat monotone.

"Go on?"

"He claims that there was a sniper team already in place at the donut shop where we had arranged the meeting," Dolf continued. "He scrubbed, bought a phone, and set up a new meeting for about ninety minutes from now."

"A sniper team?" Miguel acted shocked. But only because someone had decided to double-down on their bet, rather than let this one go.

What had Handsome Rob done to piss off someone in this building?

Again, he hoped that Esmeralda wasn't the suspect. They'd simply be doomed if she had turned.

Perhaps he'd made a mistake, sending her, but there was one way to be sure that his instincts were still right on things. She'd bring him in safely, or not.

"I have a problem, Miguel," Dolf said bluntly. "As far as I can tell, communications with Segura are compromised. And inside this building somehow. Rob's next meet might be a set-up for him as well, because someone had to have told the snipers where to find him last time. Too many people are in the loop right now."

"What do you suggest?" Miguel asked calmly.

"We need to activate some of our clandestine defector protocols," Dolf said. "Use them right here. Small team. Isolated communications. Outside the building. At least until we can get Rob to safety."

"How many people may have known the contents of the

first call?" Miguel asked, echoing the previous conversation with Esme.

He'd known Dolf for more than a decade. Promoted the man to Chief when his predecessor retired. Alcazar should be beyond reproach.

But so should everybody else.

"Too many," Dolf grimaced. "With your permission, I'll take a small team out into the field with me right now and see if we can cut things off."

"Okay, I can understand the need," Miguel said. "What about headquarters?"

"Rob was on an open line when he said snipers on a rooftop, so whoever heard has to know they might be blown," Dolf said. "Activate the Internal Investigations Team and have them start ransacking lives. If nothing else, all the noise and chaos should open me a wedge to get things done today. Once Rob is safe, we can do other things under more controlled circumstances."

Miguel considered his options. Those teams eventually reported to Stansfield, in his role as Chief of Staff, to keep even Miguel somewhat isolated. Better that way, as Internal Investigations were beloved by none, a fief almost unto themselves.

"And you?" Miguel asked after a moment.

"I'll grab a team, including Esme's favorite field nerd, and walk out the front door for a while," Dolf brightened. "We won't check in until we have Rob safe, or sundown, whichever comes first."

"Be available if Stansfield or I need to reach you," Miguel said. "Otherwise, you've got twelve hours. Use them wisely."

Dolf grinned and bounced out of his chair, nodding only as he turned and then the man was gone out the door, leaving a slightly-bewildered Ben standing in the doorway.

"I'll need Brightmeadow-Gates next," Miguel ordered his assistant.

Ben nodded and pulled the door shut, leaving Miguel alone with his thoughts.

The streets of Puerto Peñasco were certainly going to be messy today, with at least three teams all looking for one agent on the run, and trying not to run into each other in the process of hunting the man. But the hallways were also going to be messy, if he unleashed Stansfield's hounds.

Miguel's Chief of Staff arrived within minutes. No doubt he had heard the contents of Segura's call and drawn his own conclusions. A leak was a dangerous thing in this business. The wrong information out there could badly compromise agents and even damage the government.

Miguel had prided himself on how little the organization had leaked up until yesterday. Now he wondered if that had all been hubris on his part, and he was going to have to take a fall.

He considered things as Stansfield took the chair, looking almost as opposite of Dolf as one could. Tall and thin. A ring of gray hair kept short around a gleaming pate. Well-tailored suit with a tie knotted just so, where Dolf never wore a tie unless he had to, and bought off the rack.

A lifetime of living as an Ops agent, where you didn't want an enemy to have a handle around your neck in a fight, and needed to wear whatever clothing the mission called for.

Night and day.

Stansfield had brought a paper cup of coffee from the corner shop with him and sipped it while watching Miguel ruminate.

"You heard the call from Segura?" he asked.

"The contents," Stansfield nodded. "Snipers watching for him to arrive. Not ours, I presume?"

"Not that I'm aware of," Miguel said. "But we should

check the duty rosters anyway, just in case. Dolf was just here and suggested that perhaps Internal Investigations needed to begin bothering people with scanners and forensic microscopes of their lives."

"What do we know?" Stansfield asked. "Besides one of Dolf's *Cowboys* getting into trouble and miraculously escaping at least twice?"

"Either the communications net outside is compromised, or we have to suspect someone on the inside is feeding an outsider information that would get them executed when it comes out," Miguel said. "Starting now, have Data Analysis track and identify every signal that emanates from inside this building for the next sixteen hours. Run it through Research and Development and have Dillon's folks put their cryptographic computers on everything, no matter how sublime or ordinary. And track the comings and goings of everyone in the building. I won't lock us all down hard, but everyone better have a good excuse for the rest of today."

"I see," Stansfield said gravely. "And Alcazar? I presume the Head *Cowboy* will be off gallivanting about?"

"Correct," Miguel said. "He's going into the field until midnight, and will only call in when he needs to update us. Send everyone home that was called in on an emergency basis, and drop back down to the normal staffing levels for a Saturday. Dolf will coordinate his own backup as needed."

For a moment, Miguel caught a hint of a scowl so bleak and angry that it was like someone else was seated across from him, but the man's distaste for the *Cowboys on Three* was well known. Like Esme, Stansfield Brightmeadow-Gates had a quiet disdain for kinetic operations, believing that passive surveillance was a much more effective tool, most of the time.

Most of the time, the two of them were right. But only most of the time.

Stansfield nodded, composed again and sipped.

"Anything else?" he asked.

"No," Miguel said. "I'll be here dealing with paperwork for a while, and then I may head home after lunch, depending on how the next meeting with Segura goes."

"Very well, Miguel," Stansfield rose and made his way to the door, opened it, and vanished.

Ben appeared again, expectantly.

"Stansfield will be sending most of the office staff home shortly," Miguel said with a smile. "Unless you have something in particular that requires you to remain, I can certainly go down to get my own files as I need them."

He could see where Ben wanted to make excuses to stay, but he'd been called in under the same emergency communications that brought Miguel in.

"I have filing and such that I've gotten behind on," Ben supplied. "This is as good a time as any to catch up everything."

Miguel considered it and then nodded. While he didn't think that the Internal Investigations teams would find anything, he needed to be prepared. More likely, the order would cause whoever it was behind the troubles to stop talking with the outside, or perhaps make the sort of mistake that would leave them unmasked.

Miguel could only hope.

If he was wrong, the government just might order the Service to be dismantled on Monday.

18

Dodger didn't like it, but there wasn't much he could say or do as they waited in their warehouse for the call.

They'd been made somehow.

The target was supposed to be a punk who'd only been an agent for a year and a half, so he shouldn't be that good, but apparently the man was. And their principal hadn't mentioned that sort of thing to him when they got the contract.

Of course, from the language in their conversation, the principal was also a little surprised that the punk had lasted as long as he had. That was one problem with a voice scrambler. You lost so much context from tone.

At the same time, Dodger and his team were used to it, so he'd learned to read things from vocabulary.

"Seriously?" Lan asked. "Sidearms and that's it?"

Dodger shrugged. He'd run this team for a long time, so it wasn't a dominance thing. Just Lan being chirpy. He was the brainiac of the team when it came to things like that. Dodger was the brute force.

"Odds are, the other side will have at least one team in

there running interference," Dodger said. "Maybe two, but we won't know until we've got eyes on and do some walking of the perimeter. They know we exist, but don't apparently know what we look like. We'll split up, with Swede four blocks away in the car. Look for hunters trying to be low-profile while they keep watch for the target."

"Will he even show up?" Arni asked. "If he knows it's a trap? I'd toss some raw meat into the circle and let the sharks have a go at each other, if I was him."

"That's why we're doing it this way," Dodger said. "Our principal doesn't figure we can actually take a shot without significant risk, but if they're looking outward for snipers, they might miss us in the middle. Worst outcome, we can track them from the meetup and maybe get a shot at the target later."

"Feels like we're pushing our luck on this one," Lan countered. "What happened to hit twice or walk?"

Dodger didn't like having his own rules thrown back in his face, but he couldn't really argue that one. They'd be going for their fourth try next.

Eventually, their luck was bound to run out, but they'd gotten paid good money for this operation. Dodger felt duty-bound to try.

At least once more.

"I don't figure the target shows either, like Arni," he said. "Kind of the height of stupid, at this point, but we need to confirm things for the paymaster, and none of the locals will know us. Not even our target, since he never got a good look in the darkness. If one of you was a dame, you'd be dressing slinky as a distraction right now, but we're just some guys who all happen to be shopping in the same neighborhood today, so strip down to one gun and one knife and leave everything else here. Then dress casual, like an office punk who has escaped the spouse for some errands and maybe a pint."

Dodger listened to the grumbling, but there was no rancor to it. Just a long-suffering team of goofball killers forced to walk out in the daylight without tactical armor or explosives.

Like spies, rather than mercenaries.

After this try, though, he'd probably have to have a long talk with the boss about cutting their losses.

Their target wasn't supposed to be that good. What other surprises were coming?

19

ROB WAS ALWAYS UTTERLY AMAZED AT SOME PEOPLE. How could anybody be so trusting, or maybe so dense, that they left their handcomm sitting on the console between front seats of their vehicle?

First off, he was on his so often that not having it in a pocket made him almost feel naked. But leaving it out in the vehicle when you went shopping? The only thing that was probably dumber at this point was leaving the vehicle running while you ran in, but it wasn't so hot or cold that someone would do that.

If they did, Rob might have considered taking it for a spin.

Right now, however, his fundamental faith in the stupidity of humanity was reinvigorated.

The vehicle was a late-model Mallory sedan. Four doors and a trunk, and not much more. Electric engines on the wheels with batteries along the bottom.

You'd think that mechanical engineers would take advantage of that to make vehicles that were more interesting, but this was a boxy rhomboid on wheels. Dull. Gray.

And some moron had left their handcomm in the front seat.

How stupid are you people?

At least the door was locked, for whatever good that would do. Nigel had provided him with a highly-illegal device designed to help law enforcement officers override a vehicle's security system in an emergency.

This was probably close enough.

He walked to the passenger door with the device palmed in one hand and aimed at the lock. It took one chirp and the lock popped open. With just the slightest glance around, Rob ducked as he opened the door and stuck his head in, smudging his prints on anything he touched. Rob grabbed the handcomm, and to be polite, locked the doors again before closing them, like he'd forgotten the first time and come back for the unit.

Elapsed time probably shorter than someone with the right fob doing it.

Nobody screamed anything as he stood up and closed the door with an elbow to not leave prints, so Rob walked across the lot and into the supermarket like he belonged.

That was the secret to being an agent. Always look like you belong. Like you have a mission. Walk with purpose, rather than slinking. Play stupid as long as you can if someone questions you, on the presumption that most folks will fall for an honest mistake if they can't prove otherwise.

Into the breakfast cereal aisle, meandering like he was indecisive about the latest sugar bomb.

Rob never ate breakfast, unless it was almost dawn and he was still awake. Brunch with mimosas was so much more civilized.

He opened the face of the handcomm and flipped open

the application for sending text messages, rather than talking. If you didn't need a voice channel, the machine would just pulse a text out to the nearest tower as it could. Harder to trace, and it wasn't like he was going to keep this phone for long.

Text only. Got your message. Burner comm. Why? Rob. Simple. Pithy. Direct.

He moved a little to his left like he was maybe having a conversation with the wife about what cereal to get for the kids.

The handcomm chirped.

Inside leak. Miguel sent me outside alone. Meet? E.

Well, duh. Snipers on rooftops, lady. Someone in the building blabbed. More than once, since folks knew where to find me this morning.

Rob smiled and moved some more, glancing up occasionally at folks as they meandered by.

Why the hell not? If it was raining, or even threatening, nobody would be out today, staying in to watch a rugby match on the screen instead.

Riverwatch Deli Dogs. 11AM. Buy one. Sit nearby. Eat. Will be in touch.

Rob checked the time at the top of the screen. Eleven was when he'd told Dolf, but there was no way he'd appear around all those yahoos. That was going to be a zoo of undercover agents, and maybe cops too just for the hell of it, all trying to look innocent and low-key. At least the merchants selling coffee would do good business today because of him.

Noted.

Now was the hard part. If this was her personal number, odds were it was a Service-issued device, like his spare that Nigel had tricked up. Possibly compromised, if the leak was someone other than Ms. MacTavish herself. Plus, he was talking to her on a stolen handcomm, which could be traced once someone figured out that they'd lost it.

Briefly, Rob considered asking Ahmed to walk up and sit down next to her, but if it was a trap, the man would be walking blindly into a shitstorm of trouble that he didn't deserve, regardless of how badly the man picked sports teams.

Rob figured he had enough time to use this device at least one more time before he needed to ditch it. Nobody automatically assumed a missing phone was stolen. They'd think they set it down and walked off, or maybe it had fallen out of a pocket or slid under the seat. An hour was enough time before he had to trash it.

If he was careful.

And it wasn't all a trap.

20

<hr>

Esmeralda studied the words on the screen as she sat in her living room. Wondered if she was walking into a trap, like Segura no doubt expected he was facing.

Noted.

She'd been trained as an agent, back thirty years ago when she first joined the Service. Back when she realized that she wasn't nearly vacuous and inane enough to handle actually trying to be a model as anything more than a side hobby. Most of those people had been dumber than rocks, getting by purely on beauty for the few years that it might last.

Esmeralda had owned cats that were smarter than some of the models she'd worked with.

Inside the Service, brains counted for more, especially if she didn't want to compete for one of the few slots in the Operations Inspectorate. Data Analysis was all about numbers and patterns, meaning she was one of the few people she knew actually putting her degree to work in the right field.

But she had to be a Field Agent today. And Miguel was

right. If she had turned, the Service would be doomed, but the same might be said of any of the people on the need-to-know list. Everyone privy to Segura's communications had already been vetted any number of times, and nothing had come up.

So Miguel had fallen back on their actual friendship, rather than the professional one. At least she hoped this wasn't another sly, offhand maneuver by he or Caroline to set her up on a blind date. They'd done that a few times, but always picked eligible men, rather than interesting ones.

Still, he tried, and it was always a good faith effort, so she wasn't going to complain too loudly. This was a favor in an entirely different category, but needs must, when the devil drives.

She considered how she was dressed. Long slacks in a heavy, blue cotton that showed off her silhouette without being baggy or tight. Warm enough if the weather never got out of the sixties today, rain or not. She slipped out of the silk blouse she had worn earlier and grabbed a warm gray pullover with long sleeves. At the last minute, she removed her bra as well, knowing that she'd have to later, if she wanted Segura to trust her at all. Too easy to hide things in the fabric architecture, either weapons or transmitters.

Esmeralda caught her image in the bathroom mirror and paused. Fifty-one. Long blond hair down to her shoulder blades with waves of natural curl and streaks of gray and white coming in where she'd never bothered to dye it. Just as long and lean as she'd been thirty years ago when she had modeled. She could still wear those outfits, although the tops might be a little tighter than they used to be.

She pulled the shirt on and tucked it in so that she could add a holster over her left kidney, where a rain shell would cover it. The holster was tiny because the weapon was small enough to hide in the palm of her hand when she made a fist. Holstered, because it would make a strange lump in her outer pocket, but then she decided that a single woman out in the park today might carry such a personal protection device like that, so she untucked her shirt and grabbed her jacket, slipping the beam stunner into the pocket.

Rain was a strong possibility, so she grabbed a hat off the coat tree by the front door as well. It had a long brim only in the front, with an open spot in the back where she could pull her hair through and keep it out of her way.

Again, looking in the mirror, she was suddenly at least twenty years younger.

Hopefully, that was good enough that nobody would recognize her, especially as she normally dressed so much nicer for work.

The place Segura had suggested was in the middle of nothingness, next to two flat pitches for games or picnics, right at the intersection where the sidewalk between them met the one running along the river. She'd be completely in the open, but that was the point.

If she had brought any help with her to this meet, they would have to be extremely far away to not be noticed, either across fields or parking lots. Alternative, they would have to fly so high that they'd be relying on infrared sensors to see through the low clouds.

She supposed that this was about as good as Segura could arrange, if he wanted to get her more or less alone.

And she had her palm stunner if she needed it.

21

Esmeralda parked her skimmer in a mostly-empty lot and looked briefly around. There was a wind coming up, but the rain was holding off for now. Chilly, but dry.

Good enough.

She exited and looked around again, before settling her cap and making her way past the apartment complexes on the river towards the pedestrian boulevard alongside the shore as the water finally exited the scrublands and drained into the sea.

Not many people around, not that she blamed them. At least the hot dog stand was doing some business this morning, although it appeared to be mostly coffee and other hot drinks for folks out walking, rather than food.

Segura's instructions had been specific, so she decided to splurge a little, getting one with a little marinara sauce and mozzarella cheese melted over it. And a bottle of sweet tea, just in case he left her sitting here for a while, while he tried to decide if it was safe to approach.

Hopefully, nobody else had followed her from her home, playing a hunch that she was up to something today. Miguel was only one who knew, and her staff had instructions today to report directly to either Dolf or Miguel, so the need for anyone to talk to her should be low.

Esmeralda found a nearby bench and sat, munching her dog carefully so she didn't end up wearing it. A few people wandered by, but nobody had put together a pickup rugby match, so she had most of the area to herself.

It left her feeling rather exposed, in more ways than one. She had no backup other than the comforting weight of the palm stunner in her pocket and the man selling brats this morning.

There was so much that could go wrong.

She took another bite and then drank some tea, feeling the chilly breeze want to cut through her jacket, but she had it closed up halfway, so it was just messing with her ponytail.

Esmeralda finished her brat and looked around while she drank more tea, wondering if that would be enough for Segura, or if this was all just the same wild goose chase she suspected Dolf's people were facing across town.

Her handcomm chirped.

Selfie with the stand in the background?

She recognized the number as the one Segura had used earlier, so she maneuvered herself to show the vendor's stand from where she sat over one shoulder.

As proof-of-life photos went, that was a pretty good way to ensure that someone was where they were supposed to be. She hoped the lack of makeup wouldn't make her look too gaunt and washed-out today.

Esmeralda sent the picture back and waited.

Excellent. Now get in your vehicle and drive to Northhenge Mall for more instructions.

So, it was going to be a scavenger hunt today? Fine.

She had to give Segura some credit for paranoia, since he'd already come close to dying at least twice today that she knew of. Having a relative stranger out there as potential bait for a third trap would not make him particularly forthcoming.

Esmeralda shrugged and rose, tossing her paper and the bottle into a recycling can as she walked by the hot dog vendor and cut back across the fields to her car.

For a moment, she almost forgot that there was anybody else in the world, since she could only see a few walkers in the extreme distance, and nobody that appeared to be following her. She put her head down and grumbled a little, but it had been a pretty good dog, and she supposed that she would need the energy if this charade was going to run on for a while.

Across the pitch, she cut through the parking lot to the mid-rise tower of flats that either had a fantastic view of the river itself on three sides, or the city from the east, where you could watch a pretty sunset most nights.

Nobody was around until a man suddenly stepped onto the walkway from one of the buildings. Esmeralda had her hand in the pocket of her jacket with the stunner wrapped up, just because, but she did a double-take when she realized who it was standing there.

Roberto Segura.

A little disheveled, and extremely disreputable. Holding a pistol in one hand pointed right at her from about twenty meters away.

Esmeralda froze, but Segura gestured for her to walk closer with his free hand. A polite one finger crooking and something of a smile on his face.

No words were spoken.

She took a shallow breath and willed her legs into motion again.

She had come all this way to meet this man. The message about the mall was obviously a trap to lure any watchers she had away while he intercepted her at the moment when everyone relaxed.

Rather well done, even by her standards.

If only someone else was watching over her.

Esmeralda had only her own wits and experience at this point. If her hand came out of her pocket with the stunner, Segura looked like he would shoot her without blinking.

When she got about four meters away, he finally broke the silence.

"That's close enough for now," Segura commanded in a quiet, hard voice. "Right hand only out of your pocket without anything in it, please."

She hesitated for the blink of an eye.

"I will shoot you if I have to," he said simply.

For a playboy agent wannabe in the mold of Jorge Royo, Roberto Segura looked remarkably like a stone killer this morning.

Esmeralda obeyed, bringing her right hand out into the wind.

"Thank you," Segura continued. "Left hand now, without the weapon, please."

How did he know she was left-handed? Or that she was armed? Or was he just playing a hunch?

How good of an agent was Segura, when she hadn't realized it?

Had anybody realized it?

Miguel had. As had Royo. Food for thought. Both were men of impeccably high standards.

"Thank you," Segura finally smiled. "Now the bad part. I'm going to need to frisk you, so please step into my closet and try not to be too terribly offended."

At least he was asking nicely, and acting like a professional, rather than some dime store hoodlum from a gangster vid.

Esmeralda stepped closer and Segura backed away at the same speed, into what looked like a maintenance closet. No, it was a riser room, she could see the pipes along one side.

Segura was closer to her now, if she wanted to do something incredibly stupid and get herself killed.

She just watched him. Segura wasn't that much taller than she was, which was itself rare, as she was just a shade under six feet tall. Most men were eye height or shorter around here.

He gestured with the open hand, keeping the pistol centered on her sternum.

"Remove your jacket and this will go as quickly as it can," he said simply. "You face this wall on my right. Hands above your head against the concrete. Feet shoulde- width apart. I'm going to touch you in ways that are extremely impolite and I'm going to put my pistol away first. If you do anything rash, I'll probably have to punch you in the face, or break your neck, and I'd rather not, okay?"

All very professional. Nothing at all personal about the violence he might unleash. She kept telling herself that.

This was the best way.

She kept telling herself *that*, as well.

Esmeralda let her jacket slide to the floor silently and assumed the position against the wall. She tracked Segura by his cologne, as he appeared to be completely silent.

The beep surprised her, until she recognized it as the same sort of scanner she'd taken into Miguel's office earlier. Perhaps the same model.

Again, taking no chances.

"I'm going to take your hat off first," he announced, in the least sexy disrobing monologue she could imagine.

Hopefully, that was all she'd end up losing right now.

She nodded, and felt a hand take hold of the brim of the hat and ease it up and back, sliding it over the ponytail and dropping it nearby on the floor after what she presumed was a quick look inside.

"Now I'm going to grab hold of your hair, so you can't move suddenly without getting hurt," Segura said. "This is as much for your benefit as mine. Say yes if you understand me."

Esmeralda suppressed the growl. This was too much like the beginning of a sexual assault, but she'd known she'd have to go through something like this earlier, when she left her bra at home.

Like the hat, too easy to hide electronics in it and set a trap for Handsome Rob.

"Yes," Esmeralda forced herself to say calmly.

"Thank you," Segura was close enough to breathe in her ear almost now. "If there was a better way, I would have taken it, Ms. MacTavish."

A big hand ran up her neck and into the hair on the back of her head like a lover might, tangling with great strength but not pulling or pushing.

Just confining her in place, and making it easy for Segura to pull her over backwards or slam her face into the cold, cement wall if he wanted to.

She concentrated on breathing evenly and not lashing out at the man, verbally or physically.

Miguel and Segura would both owe her after this.

"Now I'm going to touch you in places I would never under other circumstances, Ms. MacTavish," he said. "My apologies in advance, and again when I'm done, but it is necessary. Are you prepared?"

"Yes," she managed to say easier this time.

It helped that he was using her surname, rather than her first name or even a nickname. Kept it on more of a professional basis.

She'd heard some of the playboy stories about Roberto

Segura. Mrs. Jones seemed especially impressed with the man.

And all that entailed.

A hand landed on her right hip and rested there for a second, like a lover walking up behind her. She'd untucked her shirt, so his hand was warm when it suddenly found the cold skin across her stomach, just above the line of her pants as it dipped ever so slightly in.

He was breathing close to her ear now.

In any other circumstances, they might be dancing erotically, but it was all she could do not to headbutt the man right now. Or bite him.

Which was probably why he had hold of her head and could control her movements.

"I know," he whispered. "I'm sorry. And it will get worse, but it will be over quickly."

The hand moved all the way to the other hip across her skin and the top of her panties, looking for a knife or holster, she supposed. Then it withdrew and went across the small of her back.

"I'm going to have to touch your breasts now, to check your bra," he said.

"I'm not wearing one," Esmeralda snapped.

"Oh?" he sounded surprised, but the hand went up her back instead of around the front, all the way to her neck inside the shirt, finding only skin.

"Okay, that's good enough," he said. "Now both arms and then both legs and we're done. Take a breath please."

She'd stopped. He could sense it, apparently.

Esmeralda contained her rage and sucked air down into her belly.

"That's better," Segura said. "Thank you."

That damnable hand went under her right arm, over the

shirt, and down to her wrist carefully. Then it retracted and went to her hip again.

"I need you to bend over while keeping your arms up," he said. "I'll keep you from falling as I check your legs."

Again, he did. Controlled her every moment, but ran down the inside of her legs no more and no longer than was necessary to check the inside of both thighs, and then down her leg as she bent forward, sticking her ass up into the air like an exotic dancer on the stage.

Around the ankle, and then across to the other and up. Left arm and he was done.

She'd been violated, but not even as bad a nurse setting her up for the annual physical before instructing Esmeralda to disrobe for the doctor.

"I'm sorry," Segura said. "There was no other way. I'm going to remove my hand from your hair, but it may be tangled, so please bear with me patiently so I don't hurt you. Okay?"

"Yes, fine," she growled.

The wind had done a number on the ponytail, and removing the hat had just let it stay that way. Segura released the tension in his fingers and pulled them outward slowly, like a lover might comb through her hair, rather than withdrawing down and pulling harshly on anything.

Then his smell was gone. No more cologne in her ear.

"Thank you," Segura said. "I'm sorry, and will continue to apologize for as long as you think necessary. You can turn around now, Ms. MacTavish."

He was holding her hat out to her when she did, so Esmeralda took it and placed it on her head for now. Her handcomm and palm stunner were in his hand.

"So what the hell is going on?" he asked.

Like she knew.

22

———

Rob considered the cold, beautiful woman standing across from him in the riser room, like a granite statue erected to mark a mighty victory in some long forgotten war.

Unlike most of the women he'd ever known who looked like they wanted to kill him, Esmeralda MacTavish probably could. He was keeping her handcomm and the little female-sized stunner he'd taken from her pocket until he was sure she wouldn't knock him down and cut his throat.

If that day ever came.

"I don't know, Segura," she replied to his question in a voice that sounded like a good mix of unfocused rage and honest confusion. "Miguel Cabrill immediately realized that we had a communications problem. He thinks we have a mole inside the Service."

"And where do you factor in?" Rob asked her, focusing on her hands and face, rather than letting his eyes linger on the breasts that were a little too outlined by the shirt she was wearing today.

Not his type of woman at all, regardless of how beautiful

III

she was. If nothing else, she was probably as smart as the last three women he'd dated combined.

Still, there was something to be said for a woman in her early fifties that was still that smoking hot, even if she might kill him.

Probably be like touching a fresh lava flow, however.

"Miguel trusts me," she replied. "Both personally and professionally. As he said to me, if I've turned, the Service probably needs to be destroyed, because everything is so compromised that *ONI* will end up replacing us."

Rob wondered if he should just defect to *Aquitaine* or *Corynthe* if something like that happened. He was too young to retire, but he'd never go to work for those yahoos over in Naval Intelligence.

Maybe he should actually take some acting classes and emulate Jorge Royo as a third-rate, washed-up actor and top-notch con artist?

"So I'm stuck trusting you and hoping that the Director isn't setting me up?" Rob asked.

"There could have been strike teams around the park, Segura," she snapped, finally letting some of the stress come out. "Taken your ass down hard regardless of how good you think you are."

"Lucky, lady," Rob snapped back. "Good only gets you so far. I've been lucky, and plan to keep riding that as far as I can. I'm supposed to be dead right now. And somebody owes me a big debt for what they did to my apartment and life."

"So are you ready to come in?" she asked. "I can get you to safety."

"Not done yet," he said. "I wanted you for the intelligence value you can provide while I plan my next step."

"And what's that?" she asked.

If he didn't know better, Rob would have thought the woman was starting to relax around him. He'd known cats like that. Wait until you thought they weren't looking, and then pounce on you.

He still had a row of tiny puncture scars on his left forearm from a woman's tabby that had done that, literally hanging in the air when he leapt up in surprise, before she pulled the cat up and gotten the claws out of his arm.

There hadn't been a second date with that one.

MacTavish had that same look in her eyes, when she didn't think he was looking.

"What's next?" he grinned. "I have a lead on the bastards that woke me up this morning. If you're on the level, you can go now and let the Director know, so he's not surprised when he sees it on the evening news tonight."

"No."

"I beg your pardon?" Rob asked, honestly surprised.

"No," she reiterated. "I'm coming with you."

"Are you nuts?"

This was Field Agent work. She was Data Analysis. If he had to guess, this woman had finished her original agent training before Rob was born. Didn't matter what semi-annual qualifying she'd done since. His training was pretty much constant when he was in town.

"The Service has someone inside, leaking information," she said. "That means someone has compromised *my* communications systems. I want to know who it is and how they did it. You think you're going to get even with whoever who shot up your flat? You have no idea what I'm going to do to the people corrupting my team."

Okay, good, honest anger, or a better actor than Jorge or Mrs. Jones. He didn't trust the woman, but maybe he could work with that.

"No strike teams headed to the mall right now?" he asked.

"None," her voice dropped down into more of a growl. "I

put myself at your mercy, Segura. Miguel wants to bring you in safely. I want blood."

"Oh that I can promise you," he replied, feeling his mouth pull back into a shark smile. "There will be killing. You ready to end someone?"

"I brought my stunner," she said.

"No," Rob shook his head. "There were five of them, but I really probably only need the one in charge to find out what I want to learn. The rest are collateral damage."

"Just like that?" she rasped. "Kill them in cold blood?"

"There's no cold blood here, MacTavish," Rob growled. "They tried to kick in my door. Did blow up my flat. Have chased me across town and shot at me. Sat outside the last meeting with a sniper rifle. We're long past playing nice. If you want to be part of this, then you'll be part of taking them down like mad dogs. That clear enough for you?"

"Yes, but you're not stopping there, Segura," she retorted with a hard smile, colder than his, if that was possible. "After you find them and keep the one alive you wanted, he's going to tell us who he works for. Then we're going after that person as well."

"That will be when it gets ugly, MacTavish," Rob reminded her. "It's got to be somebody high up at the Service, where they could control investigations to avoid having their double life exposed. Someone like you, or Dolf, or even Cabrill. Considered that?"

"You think I liked putting myself under your power, Segura?" MacTavish asked with a sneer. "Looked forward to having you pulling my hair or feeling me up so you could be sure I was clean? Is that what you think of most women?"

"No, Roxy cured me of that stupidity a while ago," Rob said, letting himself relax rather than start arguing with this woman.

She had done everything he had demanded, without

complaint. Without resisting. Could have made it much harder on him.

He could have also made it much worse on her.

"I'm trying to do this thing with the least number of innocent casualties, MacTavish," he continued. "If you come along, you might get hurt. This is Ops stuff, not Data Analysis. That sharp end of the stick that occasionally gets called in because all the easier, safer, smarter methods have failed and the Director needs a blunt instrument propelled at high speed to make a point."

"Are we going to do this or just listen to you yammer about it, Segura?" she snapped.

Rob blinked.

MacTavish was a harder woman than he'd given her credit for. All the soft beauty and lean elegance had distracted him. She was still a killing blade underneath.

Fine.

"Then you're in," Rob said. "What message did you need to send to the Director that you have made contact, but can't bring the bad boy in yet because of other problems?"

She held out her hand with a cold, stern face.

Rob took a chance and handed her the handcomm, tucking her little shock shooter into his own jacket pocket for now.

The coldness in the eyes was a glacier a kilometer deep, but she didn't say anything. Just keyed the device open.

"Text only," Rob instructed her. "Harder to track, even with our phones and your systems at the other end."

If looks could kill… But she followed his instructions, both thumbs dancing across the screen.

She held the handcomm up and turned it for him to read.

Innocent enough message, but they all had code phrases

and emergency signals embedded in their files and their memories.

The only way Rob would know for sure would be to break into headquarters right now and read her file, because torturing the information out of her looked about as possible as beating a mountain to death with a rock hammer.

Yeah, you could do it, if you had enough years and enough patience.

He didn't even have time to consider.

All or nothing.

Rob nodded at her and tried to smile.

She hit send and looked up at him.

"Now what?" she demanded.

"Now we run like hell," he replied, pulling his stolen handcomm out of his pocket and dropping it into the trashcan by the door.

23

—————

Dodger had been through all the same sorts of
tactical training as the men and women he was facing today.
There were only so many schools teaching it, and only so
many ways to do it.

Still, the opposition was pretty good at this, even if they
were handicapped by following any sort of formal rules.

Dodger had his own rules for operations, and had
worked with his men for several years. He didn't need to
work in awkward teams, or try to keep in constant
communications without looking obvious or stupid about it.

It both helped and hindered that the bakery where the
target had supposedly arranged the next meet was on
something of a market square, with a large, triangular
pedestrian area that was bounded on all three sides by little
shops with office space above them. As well as a dozen little
kiosks selling crap, coffee, or foodstuffs out in the middle.

The weather was marginal today, with the wind
occasionally gusting and twisting, but the sky wasn't sure if it
wanted to rain or not. Everyone was in jackets or raincoats,
which lent them a certain anonymity, but nobody was really

spending any time seated on any of the benches or spaces near planters where it would normally be standing room only when things were warmer and dry.

Lan had found himself a spot at a standing counter in a pirozhki shop, with a pasty, a coffee, and his handcomm. The man even looked like a tired husband sneaking some away time from the family and reading the news.

Kovalchuk was standing around with a small crowd, apparently watching a team of jugglers throw things back and forth while keeping up a running commentary of jokes.

Dodger wasn't sure where Arni had gone off to, but that was normal. Arni was the one who was dangerous in close, where you wanted to use a knife to be sure.

Good enough.

Dodger could see at least three pairs of Lincolnshire agents moving around in that *"I'm not an agent on surveillance"* mode. He presumed that the Service folk had brought at least a full field team, so there'd be two sets of others with elevation, somewhere behind the mirrored glaze above him on all three sides.

Not much he could do about those folks. Fortunately, they'd be relying on cameras instead of guns, unless the yahoo in charge had decided to bring along a sniper or two with good sight lines.

Dodger knew where he'd put folks like that, on the narrow corners of the triangle around him, but he would be too obvious himself if he stopped and studied the right places.

He was just a mook out for the morning. Running some errands downtown. Maybe stop and hit the bookstore for the latest romantic thriller. In need of a little coffee and perhaps a treat for himself first, because he'd had a hard week working for an ignorant martinet with delusions of adequacy.

It made a pretty good face. And he sort of fit right in with the others in the mob this morning.

The clientele was skewed male, which he put down to weather. Warmer, and families might come down with the kids. Cooler like this, and the missus might just send the mister out and tune the kids up with a video to keep them distracted.

At least there weren't any museums close by, so he didn't have to worry about stray pulses overshooting and hitting a mob of kids.

Dodger had a hat today to go with his rain shell. A plaid hooligan that he pulled down a little low against the breeze and prying eyes as he made his way through the crowd. It wasn't packed enough around here that he had to bounce anyone with an elbow, but he still moved slowly.

A man not in a hurry, because it was his day off and all he had to look forward to this afternoon was a pint and a match later. He turned and headed towards the bakery that was ground zero for all the stupidity going on today. At least the target had good taste in food.

Dodger walked in and tracked every face in here against undercover agents probably doing the same thing he was. Then maybe things would get a little worrisome.

But first, a blueberry danish.

24

———

Dolf didn't like it. Not one damned bit.

But he was in charge, and he'd be well and truly damned before he'd let someone else run this operation. Too much could go wrong.

Had gone wrong. The whole day had been one long screw-up, as far as he was concerned.

How in all the possible hells had they gotten here?

His place was behind a fourth floor window with a good view from the apex of the Julian Square. The building had a security guard in the lobby downstairs, mostly because it was on such a crowded fronting and office folks might come in on the weekend.

It was amazing how quickly people moved when you flashed the right credentials and invoked planetary security.

So, conference room with a long table. His team had moved all the electronics underneath, after taking a photo, so folks coming in on Monday might never know anything had happened. In their place, donuts, bagels, and coffee from a chain closer to headquarters that happened to be on the way.

Nobody knew how long they'd be here.

Dolf had brought Matilda with him, rather than leave her back at HQ. She was MacTavish's expert on comm systems, and had established a fast routing back to the river for when Segura called in.

Dolf didn't expect Rob to do anything silly like that, but he needed to cover all bases. Everything had already gone so wrong today that they'd be months doing procedure assessments and fixing things.

The room was as clean as Matilda's scanners could make it, and he had unplugged everything from the walls and floor just to be double sure. Right now, she was at the head of the table like a tiny queen. Five foot tall. Ninety-nine pounds. Petite.

Until then she opened her mouth and all the brains became evident.

Dolf had a headset on, as did she and the two watchers at the edges of the window with optical scanners focused on the crowd. Everyone down there had earpieces in and throat mics. It wasn't ideal, but there hadn't been time to do things properly, and the crowd wasn't that bad.

Two people walking along and murmuring to each other would hopefully not be identified as having a conversation with God.

"Team one, check in," Dolf called out, keeping the time in his head.

"The new Wilson bestseller is in," Dolf's agent replied, obviously not breaking character while checking out the bookstore.

Good enough.

"Team two," Dolf continued.

"What do you think about the blue shirt?" a man's voice came over the line.

Dolf had them all trained well. Actors who could convey things over an open line that told him what he needed. Two was in the department store at the longest corner, obviously on the ground floor in the men's section, pretending to be a husband and wife, or a couple out on a date.

"Team three?" Dolf finished the round.

"Should someone call the police about a pick-pocket working the crowd?" her voice came back quietly.

"Negative, three," Dolf said. "Already too many variables going on here. Don't need the added excitement of stepped-up police patrols as we try to rescue our agent. Probably spooks everyone and we have to start over this evening if that happens."

"Understood."

Dolf watched the crowd. He could see perhaps one hundred and fifty people below him, with another third or so coming and going in the shops, plus however many people might be in the department store right now.

Everything looked a little thin, but that couldn't be helped. Less cover for his agents. Less cover for whoever might be causing Rob troubles.

Hopefully, enough space for Rob to make a quiet entrance, get extracted, and everyone could get home.

Nobody had to get hurt today.

Well, maybe.

"Sniper one, what is your status?" Dolf called out.

"Ready to engage," a woman called back. "No targets identified."

"Sniper two?"

"Green here."

Dolf checked his watch, just in case, but it was still ten minutes until the hour. He had no idea if Rob would arrive early, on time, late, or not at all. Or if anyone else was out there hunting his agent.

There were contingency plans in place for this sort of

thing, but they hadn't had to resort to anything that drastic in years. Was that a sign of good luck or bad? Complacency?

Did they need to run this sort of thing as a training exercise every year or two, just because it had come up as a problem?

At least he was prepared to escalate things to the sort of level that would make the evening news.

"Scout one, what is your status?" Dolf asked aloud.

"Heavy team is prepared for rapid insertion," the agent in charge called back. "We are seven blocks away on a high rooftop with a view all the way around and do not see anything disturbing. We can be on the ground in thirty seconds shooting."

"Very good," Dolf said.

He couldn't pace in here, so he walked over to the table instead to grab himself a danish and poured some coffee. Technically, he shouldn't be here either, but it was his operation, damn it.

His agent in trouble.

His Service facing a crisis.

Better to overplay this hand than live to regret someone else's decisions in the split second when shooting might become necessary.

Monday, there were going to be some changes in the organization.

25

DODGER COULD RELY ON LAN, KOVALCHUK, ARNI, AND
Swede. Their asses would go down just as fast as his would, if
it came to that. And vice versa.

That was what made the strength of his team so much
better than the Service agent goodie-two-shoes punks
walking around and trying to be invisible.

Like the couple that had walked in seven minutes early,
gotten a pair of coffees and a glazed cinnamon roll to split.

Dodger had gotten double lucky with this store. It
wrapped L-shaped as you came in the door, with a display in
the window that could be changed out and a long glass case
down your left, leading you to pay at the very back. All of the
tables in here were set for two-top, on the presumption that
if you were here, it was a break with a friend, rather than a
meal.

He'd managed to score the table at the very back, just as
some lawyer pimp had folded up his computer and put it
away. Probably had been working all morning and was now
going off somewhere more important. Not that Dodger
cared, except that he was seated exactly next to the one

restroom, with the whole of the shop in front of him, and behind him wasd the corridor for employees into the back and out into an interior hallway inside the building, if he needed to shoot someone in here and then run like hell for cover.

He'd lied to the others, and brought a petite smoke grenade with him, just in case. Distraction at the right moment, as it were, when smoke and a man yelling FIRE would cause a stampede.

There was no extra credit for neatness when assassinating someone.

So he sat with about half his danish in front of him and sipped coffee with his off-hand. His right hand wasn't out of sight in a pocket, being obvious about drawing a pistol, but he could get to it quickly.

Right now, the faux couple agents were working hard at not being obvious. Sitting face to face with untouched coffee in hand while the male facing Dodger's way pulled small pieces off the roll and ate them rather daintily.

First Rule of Cover: If your cover calls for coffee and a pastry, then stay in character, damn it.

He considered being professionally offended, but decided to take advantage of their crass stupidity instead and let them track the crowd for him. He could watch the female agent's back and bottom under the cover of appreciating it, waiting for her body language to change if she saw the target. Or figured out that those two weren't alone in here.

More bites of the danish. Almost gone now, but he had coffee and took a sip to stay in character. Must be getting close to a lunch rush of some sort. Maybe the staff had turned on an outside blower and whooshed freshly-baked bread smell over the crowd, because suddenly there were six people in line and more queueing up at the door.

Like grandma had just pulled cookies out of the oven.

The target wasn't visible in line, seat, or window. The noise was picking up a little, to the point that the agents could probably talk to their controller, wherever they were, without anyone at the next table overhearing.

He would have liked to have been able to listen in, but they would be scrambled on a side frequency, and the only way that could have been hacked would have been for Dodger's principle to give them the right gear.

Plausible deniability went right out the window when you did that.

The female agent was getting antsy. Turned both ways to quick scan the crowd, but male agent wasn't locked on Dodger right now, and she couldn't see without turning completely around like an owl to look.

Dodger pulled out his handcomm and opened it to check the time. And see if he had any messages, like a normal mug out and about. Maybe check the news.

Nothing from the others, so all was running as well as could be expected.

He went back to just people-watching. Nothing too terribly obvious or exciting, except that he'd have to shoot the male agent first, then the female, if trouble broke out, but the male looked to be a younger agent paired with a more senior woman to at least make them look less visible in the field.

Dodger sipped his coffee and waited like a trapdoor spider.

26

———————

ROB TOOK A DEEP BREATH AS THEY EMERGED FROM THE apartments into the parking lot where MacTavish had parked her skimmer. He kept telling himself that it was only his imagination painting a bullseye on his back as he walked next to her.

They weren't holding hands, but were close enough to be *together*. She still had that exquisite rage in her eyes, but had largely kept the verbal sniping to herself. He practiced having a thick skin, knowing she'd describe today in great detail later, so everything better make him look good.

Or at least professional.

They walked to the skimmer and she chirped the locks open. Rob got into the passenger seat like it was perfectly normal, and hoped that there wasn't someone hiding in the back seat somehow, with a knife or a garrote.

MacTavish got in and looked over at him.

Didn't say anything, just stared for a long moment before she put on the safety harness and adjusted it. He did the same.

Commercial skimmers were almost as easy to drive as

ground vehicles, but cost more and required far more skill and patience. You didn't have ground to use as friction if you needed to jam on the brakes, and could do weird things with the repulsors as you moved.

"Where are we going?" she asked as she brought the flight systems on line.

"Out of the lot and west," he replied, evading a good chunk of the answer she was seeking.

Trust only went so far.

Rob checked his handcomm and wondered how much fun everyone was having at the bakery right now without him. Not that he minded not being there, but he did make a note to make it up to everyone later. This was still supposed to be his day off.

"That's it?" MacTavish asked.

"Yes," Rob said. "Need to know, and you don't. Not yet."

There could always be a flyer above them, tracking the car from invisibly high.

Nothing he could do about that but to make their lives miserable, too.

She powered forward and out onto the street. Traffic wasn't bad for a Saturday.

"Left at the next light, then in the far lane to turn left again not long after that," Rob said as they got closer to his destination.

One of the less nice neighborhoods. Not bad, per se, but not where rich and beautiful people like Esmeralda MacTavish would live. Or even visit, unless she was slumming.

A step down from where Handsome Rob lived, just because he preferred a middle-class cover identify if asked. These were the blue collar backbone of the city. Dockers. Fishermen. Machinists. Mechanics.

Jobs that really couldn't be automated out of existence

because they required both brains and muscle in equal amounts. Pay was enough to put your kids into better educational programs, give them as many options as they wanted.

MacTavish made the turn in silence. Not even grumbles under her breath, for once.

Got into the far lane and puttered along as traffic started to sag a little. All the folks coming in from the edges for a day in the city. Plus folks out running errands that they took a vehicle, rather than having to walk somewhere in the rain later.

"There's a car coming out of a parking spot on your left," Rob said, spotting the lights. "Take his spot. We can walk from here."

Again, no grumbles. No sidelong glares that ever made it as far as her eyes, but Rob could see it in her hands on the controls. Smell it burning underneath the lovely rose and lilac perfume she had worn today.

She parked and killed the lifters. Turned to him. Scowled mightily.

"We're going into a pub nearby to talk to a friend of mine," Rob explained quietly. Calmly. Like you might when facing a bear roused midwinter. "Then we might go see some other folks about interior decorations."

"I'll need a weapon," she said pointedly.

"He'll get you one," Rob answered. "Something far more lethal than your stunner."

"How can you be sure?" MacTavish asked bluntly.

"He's a friend," Rob said. Reconsidered. "As much of a friend as this job allows, anyway. I had to tell him what I did for a living this morning, since I called him and you might have traced it. He still wants to help."

Her face changed. Rob couldn't tell what she was thinking, but something had gone a different direction from where it had been a moment ago, like a wave receding back out to sea after crashing on the sand.

"Okay," she said simply.

Rob watched her open her door and climb out. He was surprised, because he had been expecting another argument, but she unbuckled and moved.

It wasn't like he was holding her against her will and needed to stop the woman from getting away. Hell, it would be helpful if she did, if only because he still didn't trust that she could kick in a door firing at anything that moved. Roxy was still the best at that.

Rob shrugged to himself and joined her on the curb, turning right and glancing over as he started to walk. She kept up easy enough, with legs longer than his and a hard look on her face.

The kind that didn't invite catcalls as she walked. Not unless you enjoyed bleeding.

Just because he was already too keyed up, Rob walked right past the front door of the place without twitching. Crossed at the corner. Looped over two blocks, down three, back four, and came in from the door on the alley where the cooks were out back having a smoke.

"Lunch order coming?" one of them glanced up at Rob with a smile.

"Soon," Rob replied breezily. "She's eaten, and I need to talk to a man about a horse, so you got time."

"Good to know."

Rob pulled open the back door and slid into the gloom, MacTavish one step behind him like an angry shadow.

"You know those men?" she whispered.

"Faces," he said. "I'm regular enough. The key is looking approachable enough to put people at ease. Then they'll talk to you."

He felt her nod more than anything, eyes scanning the crowd as he moved.

Ahmed was at the bar, with a good view of a screen showing an East Coast match that had already started.

"Lunch for two?" the woman at the front asked as she turned to watch them approach.

"Booth, please," Rob smiled at her. "My buddy got here already, and wasn't expecting us to join him this early."

"Right this way," she said, grabbing menus and doubling them back.

Rob caught Ahmed's eye as they did, and nodded. Ahmed grabbed a mostly-full beer and stood up off his stool, turning once to scan the entire place before making his way close.

Rob got MacTavish seated on the inside of the booth and slid in next to her, almost like this was a date or something. Although the next time he touched this woman, Rob fully expected to pull back a bloody stump instead of a hand.

He got enough into the booth to not fall out, but nowhere close enough to actually touch her at any point. She gave him a strange look at his behavior, but kept her silence and her cool, which was all Rob really needed.

Ahmed McIntyre al-Inverness was tall and skinny. Rob's weight, four inches taller. He had a Arabic background so his skin was as dark as Rob's but more brown and less red. Plus, he would need to shave again in the afternoon if he was going someplace nice enough to dress for it.

Tonight probably didn't count.

The cop slid in across from them with a reserved smile.

"Ahmed, this is Mac," Rob introduced them. "No last names. She demands to help later, when we go visit our friends."

Rob kept his grin to himself as Ahmed checked the woman out, at least the top half he could see from where she was sitting. Her jacket was open just enough to distract. The hat still contained her hair back in the ponytail. No makeup, but Rob didn't think she needed any. Softer-looking hands from typing all the time rather than punching things.

Thirty-something babe, out for a beer with her boyfriend. Sure.

Ahmed smiled like he would at any pretty girl he met in a place like this. Rob didn't feel like warning him how dangerous the woman thought she was, if she wanted to be here.

"Mac," Ahmed oozed honey over the name. "Pleasure to meet you."

"I'll need a class-three pulse pistol with a laser-dot aiming mechanism on the barrel," she replied just as sweetly. "Rob here tells me I'll need to be killing people later."

Rob did grin as Ahmed's face fell. Smiled as the cop turned to look at him now with something like disbelief.

Of course, he hadn't mentioned to her that Ahmed was a cop, just like Ahmed should have drawn the obvious conclusion from this morning's conversation that Mac was most likely another spy like him.

"Got anything useful in the safe at home?" Rob asked innocently, like this sort of thing happened every day.

The waitress rescued Ahmed by coming for drink orders. Rob got hot tea. Mac got coffee. Ahmed continued to nurse a beer that had barely suffered any drinking.

"You're serious?" Ahmed asked her once they were alone again.

"You a good enough killer to come with us?" she replied with a bright smile on her face.

Rob almost felt bad that Mac was taking all her anger at him out on Ahmed instead, but he supposed that those two would need to establish a solid working relationship on very little, and she obviously wasn't feeling like playing a bimbo today. Or a damsel in distress that the big, bad cop and spy needed to rescue.

"Yeah, maybe," Ahmed finally managed after sputtering futilely a few times.

"There you go," she smiled at both of them and flipped open her menu.

Ahmed's pupils were a little dilated now, so Rob smiled and flipped his menu as well.

Not even remotely the way he'd expected this conversation to start, but Rob could say that about most of his day already anyway, so he didn't feel like he was losing ground.

Not gaining much, but not backsliding either.

He had a spy who thought she was dangerous, and a cop who thought he was subtle.

Idly, Rob wondered if that was enough to do the job, except that there had been four shooters and a driver earlier. He'd probably need something a little more serious if he was planning on taking them all on.

There was no way to call in a heavy team from the Service for this. Too much risk of a leak. And no way to ask the local cops for one of their strike teams, because somebody would absolutely talk.

He really missed not having Mrs. Jones here right now. Roxy was quite possibly the most dangerous human with a gun Rob had ever met. And he had spent nearly a decade being trained by professional killers how to do that job. Jorge Royo was no slouch either, and always got bonus points for carrying an unspilled martini in his off hand. Even Longbow never got enough credit, once Rob had finally looked up a count of the people the musician had killed in a career of being team medic.

It was a frighteningly high number.

Rob had killed exactly one person to date. And that was

just putting down a rabid dog after Roxy had already shot the woman.

Today felt like maybe he was going to change that number significantly. But he was also angling for that promotion beyond Field Agent, which meant Assassin.

He just had to survive whatever grief and mayhem Saturday held.

27

———

Esmeralda had never been a *Mac*. *Esme*, to her close and dear friends. And one husband who had changed his mind about marrying a career woman and had instead run off with a bimbo.

But this was not a Data Analysis Inspectorate day.

Handsome Rob Segura had looked at her like too many men did, never getting past the chest and cheekbones. Or even worse, dismissing her as *just another nerd*.

Violence was apparently the means by which those sorts compared penises.

She'd have left them to their juvenile antics, these two punks, except that Miguel had asked. Had pretty much proven that someone inside the Service was leaking information.

Had compromised *her* communications systems and made *her* look like a fool.

She could become a *Mac* to solve that sort of issue.

That sort of person.

She sipped at her coffee and studied Ahmed. He looked like a cop. Practically gave off cop pheromones as he sat there. Not a bad looking chap, but Ahmed suffered when sitting close enough to Segura for comparison.

Segura, like his mentor Royo, had that square jaw and thick hair that would age gracefully for decades, trading rough for roguish as he went. And he had charisma, from learning how to keep things understated.

She decided that it could have gone much worse, there in that tiny room. She'd steeled herself for it, but Segura had managed to keep things polite. Mac was just glad she'd never gotten a nipple pierced in college when that had been a fad. She'd have had to take it out, or suffered a *close-inspection* to make sure it didn't have any electronics.

Mac made a mental note as she read the menu to talk to Dillon Vergrue, Head of Research and Development, to see what sorts of things his folks might come up with along those lines. Most men would lose all their IQ points just seeing such a thing as a woman's nipple, and it could be hung in such a way to conceal equipment.

Invisible in plain sight, as it were.

Mac smiled at the two men and considered suggesting Prince Alberts to them. It warmed her up from all the coldness of her rage.

Segura hadn't pushed, and Ahmed had recognized the line she'd drawn, so she concentrated on her menu. From the gist of the conversation, Mac suspected that she'd need to eat something now in spite of the bratwurst, because dinner was likely to be either take out, or something grabbed at a bodega as part of a surveillance stake out.

Crap, either way.

So salad, with some chicken and shrimp for protein, plus avocado for fat. She closed her menu and studied the two silent men out of the corner of her eyes.

Segura had a pent-up rage similar to hers, but aimed at a

group of strangers. Ahmed moved like something of a wingman, gliding along in Segura's wake. Both had that loose feeling she had come to recognize around undercover agents, which just reinforced Ahmed in her mind. Police Detective of some sort.

He looked up at her now from under hooded brows. Heavy, shaggy brows that would probably look better if he found a female stylist and let her work some magic, rather than the male barber Ahmed obviously used.

"Co-worker?" he asked quietly, nodding discreetly at Segura.

Mac smiled and nodded in an off-hand way.

Let him make of that what he would. If she had access to her console right now, she could probably tell the man his ID number, birthday, and blood type, just by cracking every handcomm in the place until she found his and then extracting his entire life from the Hall of Records three seconds later.

A chill seemed to come over Ahmed. Probably finally understood what *Spy* meant.

They weren't above the law, but frequently worked outside that very law to uphold it, doing things that others might find morally and ethically squishy in the name of protecting *Lincolnshire* from the wolves at *Salonnia* or *Corynthe*. Or even *Aquitaine*, although those folks were generally benevolent.

For the most part.

"Class-three pistol?" he continued carefully, circling back to her armament request.

"Two or a four would also work," Mac smiled at him. "I prefer the three because they usually fit my hand better."

And that was what she generally qualified on at the range, although she hadn't been through a Hogan's Alley combat sim in maybe a decade.

The waitress returned and took orders, distracting everything at that point until she left.

Segura seemed calmer now. Not relaxed, but not as tightly wound.

With a jolt, Mac recognized that he'd been afraid she would lash out at him. Not that he hadn't given her reason, but he also hadn't given her a good reason.

Gentleman, when he had a reputation as a philandering playboy.

Maybe some of Royo's charm was rubbing off on the punk, after all. She turned to him with an encouraging smile.

"You said a team had been waiting for you at the donut shop?" she prompted.

Segura studied her face for a moment, like he was expecting this to be a distraction while she went for his eyes, maybe.

He blew a breath out and she could actually see his shoulders come down.

You aren't that afraid of me, are you?

But she didn't say that. Better if he had a little queasiness. Ahmed, too.

Segura nodded and turned to include Ahmed in his low explanation.

"Sniper a few blocks away on a rooftop," he said quietly. "Spotter. Two others guarding rear flanks."

"Pros?" Mac asked.

In response, Segura pulled out his handcomm and called up a set of pictures that were far crisper than his handheld could have taken. But she already knew he was a man of unseen resources. Probably something from Royo's team that had made its way to *Handsome Rob*.

She studied the image, but none of the faces were recognizable. Just their stance and equipment.

Yes, professional killers. Hired by someone she worked

with to kill Segura for reasons she didn't yet understand, unless someone from a prior mission had managed to identify Segura and put a great many disparate pieces together.

Ahmed studied it next. Segura flipped to a picture of an interchangeable ground car with a driver slumped back like he was asleep.

"That's the car," Segura said unnecessarily. "Ahmed here tracked it to an address for me."

Ah. Yes, absolutely a cop. Called in a favor with a dispatcher.

"Where?" Mac asked.

"Warehouse district," Ahmed said. "Not far from the starport. Rob thinks they have built out the interior and live there while on-planet, and normally take missions elsewhere."

She nodded. Professional mercenaries, then. A whole ecosystem of folks outside the Service, still drawing occasional paychecks when something was so dangerous, or so delicate, that you needed to do it without leaving your own fingerprints.

"Are three of us enough to take five of them?" Mac asked Segura.

He grimaced.

"No," he replied after a moment. "And I can't call your friends for help. Ahmed has offered to call a few of his."

"You got a better option?" Ahmed asked.

"I could ask some folks that would smell you coming a klick away, Ahmed," Rob turned to the cop and then smiled. "But you'd have to play nice with them."

Mac wasn't sure if a team of cops or criminals would be a bigger hassle, at least from her standpoint. Both would probably see her as some sort of lethal gun moll.

Best be lethal, then.

"I'd prefer my folks," Ahmed said, turning to her. "Any chance that your organization could smooth out any misunderstandings with my bosses later, if news of this gets out?"

"I'm here at the direct request of the Director," Mac said simply. "He owes me many favors on this, so we can extend that in your direction, Ahmed."

"Good," the man relaxed. "I can make some calls then. When did you want to do this?"

That last part was directed at Rob, so she turned to see his reaction.

"Right now, everyone is all downtown, playing tag on Julian Square," he smiled ferally. "Bad guys have probably been at this for twelve hours now, so at some point they should go home and rest. Especially if I've vanished off the grid."

He turned to stare at her now.

"Assuming I'm off the grid," he continued in a harder tone.

"Nobody but me knows where you are, Segura," she growled back at him, pushing the man back just a little verbally.

She'd cut him some slack for acute paranoia, but not much.

"Then if we can stay perfectly silent for now, I'd like to give them until around nightfall," Segura told both of them. "Just after dinner and maybe they've been too keyed up all afternoon to nap, so we catch them off-guard."

"Where should I assemble them, assuming I can gather up a *few friends?*" Ahmed asked carefully, not mentioning that they would probably all be wearing armor with *Policia* in big, white letters front and back if she had to guess.

"There's a parking lot on Twenty-Seventh and Del Mar," Rob said. "We'll meet there at six, organize, scout, and maybe hit the place, depending. Won't know until then where we're at."

Ahmed wanted to say something, but the waitress returned with food, so the conversation kind of tapered off.

Esmeralda MacTavish concentrated on becoming this *Mac* person for real as she ate, rather than just a role she had to play.

Segura and his friend were serious about possibly kicking in a door and shooting anything that moved inside.

And she was going to help.

28

——————

"Yes?" Miguel looked up as someone rapped on the
door and then opened it.

Stansfield stuck his head in.

For the briefest instant, Miguel couldn't tell if the look
on the man's face was from sucking on a lemon or
discovering a new dessert bakery. Triumph and disgust
seemed to be warring in his eyes, but never making it as far as
his mouth.

Then the look was gone and the undertaker returned.

"News from the field," he said, slipping into the room
and closing the door behind him. "Apparently the *Cowboys
on Three* did something wrong, as Segura never showed up."

Miguel glanced down and realized that it was already
noon.

"No communications from Segura?" he asked, just in
case somebody had forgotten to keep him in that loop.

"None," Brightmeadow-Gates shook his head sadly.

Not that the man had ever particularly liked Segura,
from what Miguel had seen.

Just another one of Dolf's *Cowboys*, the kind that

Stansfield didn't believe even knew how to be proper agents, like the men and women of Brightmeadow-Gates's generation.

"Esmeralda has gone home," Miguel said. "But Alicia is still on duty here, with Matilda out in the field?"

"She is," Stansfield said. "I just made sure that the canteen delivered her lunch, in case she needed to be at her console when your cowboy finally deigned call in."

"Not my cowboy, Stansfield," Miguel replied, perhaps a little churlishly. "Dolf's. Or Royo's depending on how you want to classify the man."

Again, that sharp spike of sourness in the eyes. But Stansfield Brightmeadow-Gates had had his glorious confrontations with Jorge Royo over the decades.

"As you wish," the undertaker replied in a lemony sour tone.

"Keep me posted," Miguel ordered, gesturing the man to depart and leave him to his files and reports.

Once alone, Miguel considered things in a whole different light.

Out of sheer paranoia, he pulled out one of Esme's pocket scanners and aimed it at the door where Stansfield Brightmeadow-Gates had just been standing, but nothing showed on the solid oak.

Miguel had been thinking about today and reading files as if one of Handsome Rob's enemies had somehow managed to track the man to *Ramsey* and Puerto Peñasco.

What if Segura was just a way for someone to get back at someone else? Like, perhaps Jorge Royo?

Once upon a time, Royo had been a serious thespian, well considered and relatively famous. Then a chance role in a low-budget, C-grade comedy caught the cultural zeitgeist and catapulted him into the outer reaches of the solar system for fame.

At the same time, all the serious roles had dried up and all the man could do was appear in various comedies, playing some variant of that swashbuckling hero, until Jorge Royo the actor had become subsumed in Jorge Royo, the role.

That perfect tan. The martini glass never farther away than arm's reach. The boredom at becoming a phenomenon.

It had been enough before Miguel's time at the Service to know the intimate details of how Royo had gotten recruited, but he had turned into a deep cover agent so bizarrely public that nobody believed most of the stories, and it let Royo become almost the perfect spy.

Later, Royo had recruited the ex-stuntwoman of the most beautiful woman in the galaxy, when the real Mrs. Jones decided to move on from action movies to more serious dramas better suited to a middle-aged woman who was still every man's fantasy.

Roxanne Teresa Omdahl. *Roxy.* Covername *Mrs. Jones.*

Two dashing lunatics that could fast-talk their way into almost any meeting room with suggestions of parties, flair, and the possibility of filming a movie.

Miguel had lost track of the number of people that had fallen for that swindle, and ended up victims of *Lincolnshire's Guardia Civil Interior.*

Throw in Levi Framingham and Nigel Phipps, and you had the *Can't Shoot Straight Gang,* who had cut a swath of merry destruction across *Lincolnshire's* enemies for over a decade.

And then Miguel had sent them their newest member. *Handsome Rob* Segura.

Was all this a way for some nemesis of Royo to get even with the man?

That complicated look in Stansfield's eyes took on a whole new level of meaning.

The *Cowboys on Three,* when Stansfield Brightmeadow-

Gates had come out of Data Analysis instead. Had been overlooked perhaps, when Miguel Cabrill was brought in as Director of the Service, representing a new generation of agents, when Brightmeadow-Gates was literally the last of the old breed still in the building. Had Brightmeadow-Gates taken affront at that, and never let it be public?

Miguel knew he had a spy in the building. A highly placed one, if they had escaped all the investigations that might uncover them.

Investigations overseen by Stansfield Brightmeadow-Gates.

Miguel felt the room go cold.

Furiously, he ran through all the data he had accumulated today. Nothing eliminated the man who was his Chief of Staff, while bits and pieces had marked perhaps a half-dozen others as safe enough to largely ignore.

Esme was off Miguel's list, because he had had to trust someone. She had made contact with Segura, but was following up on the investigation from that end, whatever that meant.

Dolf was in the field with a team, presumably returning here to debrief Miguel shortly on whatever had gone wrong.

Twenty other names were penciled onto the page in Miguel's head. None of them should have a reason or the resources to hire killers that were going after Segura.

Unless it was all aimed at Jorge Royo.

Everything tumbled into different piles at that point. The vast bulk of Operations lived in awe of the man and what he had accomplished. That removed most of the list, leaving folks from Data Analysis and Research and Development on a list of suspects.

Esmeralda MacTavish. Dillon Vergrue.

Stansfield Brightmeadow-Gates.

Miguel rose shakily, pocketing the little hand scanner as

he did. He made his way to the door and opened it. Ben looked up in expectant surprise, since Miguel hadn't used the intercom.

"I'm going to go down to the library to look something up, and then to the canteen for lunch," Miguel announced in as calm a voice as he could manage, hoping not to crack or otherwise betray himself, with Brightmeadow-Gates's door open just down the hall. "Depending on when Dolf gets back, he might lunch with me."

"Understood, Director," Ben said. "I'll hold the fort here."

"You do that, Ben," Miguel smiled at the young man.

He moved to the hallway and focused himself on duty and calmness as he walked past Stansfield's open door, not pausing or looking in.

To the stairs and down. The Library was where all the paper records were kept, down in the sub-basement, below even the War Room, but the walk would give him time to get his heart rate under control.

Hopefully.

He needed to look at something in Brightmeadow-Gates's file.

And possibly throw the man to the wolves.

29

Dodger let his grumpiness finally out past the calm shell he'd been maintaining, once they all got back into the car.

For a few long moments, he'd had both hands close to the pockets where a smoke grenade and a pistol had lurked, but the poor sap who had walked in had just born an uncanny resemblance to the target.

Fortunately, the man had brought along an apparent wife and two children to get pastries. Dodger didn't think the target was cold-blooded enough to sacrifice folks like that, but he couldn't be sure.

The two agents he had been watching hadn't reacted at all to the man, though. And Dodger had been watching close enough that some reaction would have been obvious, either a twitch, or the urge to immediately suppress it and go perfectly still.

Like him, the woman had perked up for a moment, and then nothing.

Just an uncanny resemblance.

Poor bastard nearly got himself killed for looking like someone else.

"Now what?" Lan asked from the front seat.

"We knew the chances were exceptionally long that we'd see him," Dodger said. "Wondering if he made us somehow at the donut shop and this was just a way to get us off his gameboard while he did something else. Need to call this in. Swede, start driving north for now, just so we're in motion."

Dodger was on the left in back, but the rank sweat smell was strong enough in here that rolling down a window and letting some of the smell out would have been nice. However, a squall line was passing through, and he didn't want to get wet.

He pulled his handcomm and triggered the recall circuit.

It took nearly thirty seconds for his phone to ring, just about the point where Dodger was getting concerned that they'd been ghosted by the person who had originally hired them.

Or cut adrift.

"No show at number two," Dodger said simply, waiting for the person at the other end of the scrambled voice to rip a pound of flesh off of him for incompetence.

Sometimes, there was just bad luck, and it felt like he'd accumulated a pile of it. Like lightning building up a charge, just before it arced into your ass and set you on fire.

"Confirmed," the reply was curt, which was probably a blessing. "There has been no contact from the target."

"Orders?" Dodger went ahead and asked, walking down the usual checklist in his head for situations like this.

Not that he'd been in one this bad in a long time, but professionals were prepared. Careful. Usually luckier, as well.

"Return to base," the person said. "I will be in touch."

And the line went dead.

Just this once, Dodger badly wanted to know if the

person on the other side of that line was male or female. The syntax and vocabulary seemed to split the difference constantly, which he supposed made perfect sense.

There was no way in hell Dodger would ever be able to identify anything about their principal at a later date. Just a comm number, a voice scrambler, and orders.

Even the money came in via magic. Dodger supposed that a bright enough accountant knowing what to look for and with a lot of official help could probably trace it all the way back to the origin, but there was no way he could.

Hopefully, they hadn't just been hung out to dry for the sin of failure.

"Lunch, then home," Dodger said as he pocketed the handcomm. "Rabbit's gone to ground and we have to wait for him to surface again."

"We screwed?" Lan asked.

"Don't think so," Dodger replied with a weary nod. It had been a long day already. "But that's why we're not going straight home. Give everyone time to relax. And if it is a trap for us, we'll approach the warehouse like a job."

Lan nodded back. Arni and Kovalchuk were generally quiet anyway, so most conversations were him and Lan anyway. Swede was a driver, not a killer.

"Chinese place out on Thirty-Third?" Swede piped up now.

Dodger nodded. A little dim sum right now actually sounded pretty good.

He couldn't tell if their principal had been wrong about the target, or bad luck had just decided to have its way with him and his team.

Dodger didn't think he was losing his touch. Certainly, they'd all been better than those Service agents trying hard to look inconspicuous, so he had that on his side of the ledger.

But what the hell had gone wrong?

30

Rob looked over at the woman as they exited the bar. Ahmed was staying behind to watch the rest of the match and make a few calls. Rob didn't want to be anywhere nearby while that happened.

Too many things could go wrong.

Had.

Might yet still.

Mac looked back like a crocodile in still water. Just two eyes above the surface and a snout full of teeth hidden below while she waited to pounce.

He turned left at random and stretched his legs. Mac fell in beside him.

Silent. Waiting.

Lurking.

He stopped outside a pawn shop and turned to study the crap on the inside of the glass, like maybe he was interested in buying a new synth. Or a pair of bright purple cowboy boots in ostrich hide.

Esmeralda MacTavish looked at him in the window's reflection.

"This is where it gets complicated," he said calmly, waiting for the argument to start.

Maybe he'd be able to pass it off as a lover's spat unfortunately playing out in public.

He'd been through a few of those.

"You don't trust me," she replied in a calm voice. "You don't want to let me out of your sight, but don't really want to spend the whole afternoon babysitting me, in case I'm the bad guy, or I'm stupid enough to call Miguel and somehow accidentally lead the bad guys to you. Close enough?"

Damn it, he kept forgetting how smart she was. How capable.

How dangerous.

"We've got at least five hours to kill," Rob said, nodding to acknowledge her observation without commenting on it. "Normally, I'd suggest a hotel room and a nap, but that's me by myself. Don't want you drawing the wrong conclusions."

She stood perfectly still, apparently thinking about those boots.

"What about a movie?" she asked. "Quiet, dark. You can relax some. We can look like an innocent couple out for the afternoon on a date."

Rob was so surprised his head snapped around to look at her directly. She had a calm, almost-smile.

"What would you normally be doing on a Saturday afternoon, if you weren't in the office?" he asked, realizing he'd hijacked the woman's life completely and didn't know hardly anything about her.

Not that they'd ever had cause to chat before, other than a polite greeting in the hallway or such.

Two total strangers, oddly met, being hunted through the streets of Puerto Peñasco by a team of professional killers.

Weren't everyone's Saturdays like this?

"If I had nothing else to do, probably I would have had

brunch down by the waterfront," Mac said, her voice subtly different from the woman he'd dragged into a closet at gunpoint and groped. "Then some shopping. Maybe a bookstore. Possibly a movie."

"You don't have anyone waiting for you to call?" Rob suddenly realized he knew nothing about her. "No family or date tonight you had to break to come rescue me?"

"Nothing," she said in a darker voice, but one that wasn't aimed at him.

Still a crocodile, but ignoring the rabbit by the water's edge while waiting for an impala to come down to drink.

He started to say something but she continued.

"I might still be seen as beautiful by some, Segura, but after forty, all the men I know are looking for a twenty-year-old bimbo. Like my ex-husband. I've known a few women, too, but none recently."

"You're supposed to turn into an old maid?" he was aghast. "You? Dumbasses."

"Who?"

"Any man or woman who wasn't chasing you down the street, Mac," he said earnestly.

"Why?"

"Oh, I don't know," Rob shook his head. "Smart. Capable. Successful. Hot. Hell, if you were a stranger on the street I'd probably be chasing after you for a comm number and a date."

She scowled, but again, the impala, not the rabbit.

"I'm old enough to be your mother, Segura," she growled.

"My pop always told me the older ones were better anyway," he retorted without realizing the words that were going to come out until they did. "They know what they want, what they're doing, and how to ask for it. Plus, they probably don't come along with any unreasonable expectations. Especially not for folks like us, who live triple lives."

"Triple lives, Segura?" She turned fully to face him now.

Rob felt a blush come on. Let it.

He turned away from her, but grabbed a hand to pull her along, like a couple out on a date or something, rather than spouses.

"There's the life where your family and childhood friends knows you are gainfully employed with some quiet corporation, but you have to lie to them about what you do and why you're always off-planet missing birthdays and holidays," he said as she caught up.

Rob noted that she didn't try to pull her hand away angrily, so at least she was willing to play along for now. He had no doubt she'd give him the sharp edge of her tongue later, when there weren't more people about.

"There's the job, where you live pretty much a monastic lifestyle, lying to everyone you meet in the field and trying not to talk too much to folks at headquarters, because most of them aren't rated to know any details except the people who keep sending you out to maybe die tomorrow."

He glanced over, but she had a pensive quietness to her, so he kept talking as they crossed an intersection. There were people on the road in sight, but the damp sidewalks were mostly bare right now, everyone largely driven inside by rain that slashed at you and then disappeared, like an assassin in the night.

"Then you have the life you try to put together outside the Service," he continued. "Where you know some folks, but can't really say anything at all to them, because that probably makes them a liability later. Ahmed only learned this morning what I do, and then only because I needed someone with no reason to betray me, who could get me information."

"No reason to betray you?" Mac finally spoke up.

"I owe him money," Rob shrugged, trying to play it off nonchalant. "And I introduce him to pretty girls who might not have an issue dating a cop. Like you, nobody's waiting up for me tonight. Maybe a few will go to a club, hoping I might be there, but that's about it."

"So a triple life?" Mac asked. "Lie to everyone you know as a matter of course?"

"Better than letting them have all your secrets," Rob retorted. "In my case, any of my secrets, because most of those get me thrown in somebody's prison. Or angry people send a posse of ex-boyfriends after me. Like today."

"Ex-boyfriends, Segura?" she asked, tugging his hand enough to draw his head over to look at her.

"Running joke in my head," he explained. "Enough ex-girlfriends who wanted to get serious, get marital. They all got together and sent all their ex-boyfriends to hunt me down. Later, when I realized I was dealing with stone pros, the assumption was that those women had pooled their resources to hire someone. Stupid, I know, but I gotta do something to keep it from getting me down."

"Does anything ever get you down, Rob?" she asked.

He noted that this might be the first time she hadn't called him *Segura* today.

"Holidays on strange planets, when I'm undercover and can't even celebrate in my own head, for fear of blowing my cover," he said. "Meeting pretty women and realizing that I'm going to have to build an elaborate fantasy life to tell them about, because I'm only ever allowed to lie to people. Easier to just keep things physical and brief. That what you wanted to know?"

"Maybe," she said in a quieter voice. "But I understand the monasticism. My ex didn't understand what was coming. Didn't know then that he would consider himself a lesser man when I was more successful than he was. Couldn't deal with that blow to his ego. Had several affairs and eventually ran off with a waitress. Good riddance."

"And nobody else was bright enough to step up?" Rob asked. "See? Dumbasses."

"You can't date inside the building," she said. "And unlike Operations, Data Analysis rarely gets out into the sunlight."

"I'm surprised random strangers don't walk up to you on the street and ask you out, Mac," Rob said honestly.

He leaned outward enough to take in her whole appearance, while making it obvious what he was doing.

"You've got it all, Mac," he concluded. "Confidence. Brains. Focus. Beauty. And a smoking hot bod."

"In that order?" she asked tartly.

"Absolutely," he said, drawing her along as they started to slow. "Pretty face and nice boobs don't last forever. And if a woman honestly thinks she's sexy, then she is. Not the ones faking it to cover up a wealth of personal issues, but the homely one who studies herself in the bathroom mirror and decides that some man is going to want to explore every inch of her body, if she decides that she likes herself. You can't fake that."

"Homely?" she snapped.

"I once dated a girl who was nobody's definition of beautiful, Mac," he fired back, careful not to let his voice rise, but they were alone as far as he could see right now. "Asymmetric face, hooked nose, almost no chin. No chest at all. Nice bottom, because she worked at it. But she was self-contained in all the good ways, and decided she was hot. Broadcast that like pheromones when she entered a room. Dumbasses didn't give her a second look. That was their failing."

"And what happened to her?" Mac asked, voice quiet but penetrating.

"Service hired me and sent me off to spy school," Rob said. "By the time I got a chance to look her up again, a year had passed, and one of the folks who'd seen me with her decided that I must have known something he didn't. They'd been married for about a month at that point. She glowed. So did he. Happily Ever After, as far as I'm concerned. That's why you surprise me by being single, Mac."

She fell silent. Contemplative.

Rob wondered if he'd finally stepped too close to the water in his enthusiasm, and that crocodile was going to have rabbit for lunch anyway. Still, he was a big boy. He'd brought it on himself.

Jorge had always taught him that honesty with a woman was going to earn you far more credit than flattery. He'd seen Jorge be blunt, but score points.

It helped that the man looked on every woman he met as a mind that needed to be seduced, rather than a nice ass to grab as she went by. Women did appreciate that.

Handsome Rob could testify.

But this creature, still holding his hand, was a different monster. Might take exception, because she was certainly in a different league than most of the women he'd ever encountered.

Jorge might have his hands full, so Rob didn't feel bad about maybe being in over his head.

He could always ditch her at the last minute. Maybe steal her car and leave her stranded while he went off to knock on someone's door. She knew the vicinity, but not the address.

"It's easier to not bother, I think," Mac said in a quiet voice that surprised Rob more than a screech of rage might have. "To just float through life and not have to spin all the yarns and lies. To just hide down in Data Analysis and read my reports."

Rob felt his mouth fall open. Closed it. Tried to find words.

He hadn't intended to wound this woman, but apparently he had. Turning into an accidental life coach or something.

"Well, you're a field agent today," he finally said, drawing her around until they were face to face.

Not close enough to kiss, but enough that he was talking to her, rather than at her.

"Maybe you'll need to talk to Dolf when this is all done," he offered. "Make him open you up a slot in Operations, so you can at least get out in the sunlight occasionally."

"Shoot people like you do?" she asked in a quiet, serious voice.

"I've killed exactly one person in this job," he leaned close enough that he wasn't telling the whole world his crimes. "And she'd already tied me up and was all set to torture me to death when my backup team blew the door in and killed everyone else in the apartment. She would have bled to death eventually, but I was angry, she was down, and I blasted her heart out with a pulse pistol. Not looking forward to upping my score later, but sometimes that's what the job calls for. And those men have made me angry enough to do it myself, rather than making someone else do it."

"Including me?" she asked, sharp and maybe a little angry.

"You don't have to join us," he reminded her. "You don't even have to be here, but you demanded a part in it. Keep that in mind. I was just kidding earlier about you having to kill people."

"I wasn't," she growled back.

In the vids, this was that moment when the music would come surging up and the two young fools would kiss, finding themselves in love despite all the differences in life and mind.

Rob still saw a crocodile in her eyes. He had no idea what she saw, because he made a living carefully lying to people with the muscles of his face.

She seemed to feel that same pull, though, because they both leaned back awkwardly at the same time. Her blush made her look sixteen, which just made it worse, because now he felt like a dirty, old man, lusting after a woman nearly twenty-five years older than he was.

"So," Rob breathed out heavily. "Movie?"

"Yes," she agreed carefully, turning away and starting to walk, her hand dragging him into her wake until he caught up.

How the hell had he gotten himself into this mess, anyway?

Oh, right. Five men with guns knocking on his door at three in the morning.

He still an accounting to look forward to later.

So did those bastards.

31

MIGUEL HAD TAKEN A SPOT IN A CORNER OF THE
canteen and made it clear, from the stern look on his face,
that everyone else should sit elsewhere. Or perhaps get their
lunch to go and head back upstairs to eat at their desk.

Dolf looked a little nervous as he entered and noted the
ring of empty tables that Miguel's glare had created. A
moment later, the man squared his shoulders and walked
over to the folks nervously serving food.

Most days when Miguel came down here, he was all
bonhomie, using this as a chance to extend the open door to
any employee who had the brass to sit with the ultimate boss
and chat.

You occasionally learned some interesting tidbits
that way.

Today, most of the staff were off having a weekend
anyway, and the few on duty knew that something big and
hairy was up, even if they didn't know all the details.

Lunch today was a choice of sliced chicken breast, with
bowtie noodles in red or white sauce on the side, or meatloaf
with mashed potatoes and gravy. How the staff had known

that comfort food would be optimal, Miguel didn't know, unless all the lights on and foot traffic in the halls before dawn had alerted the kitchen manager.

He would ask at some point, though, and probably put a little, gold star next to the woman's name. This was not the day for spicy Pad Thai noodles or chili.

Dolf approached with the meatloaf, two slices of white bread perched on the side with lemonade.

Miguel gestured for him to sit and worked on finishing his pasta.

He studied the Ops Chief as the man carefully cut and organized his meatloaf, using the bread to make a sandwich he could stuff quickly into his mouth after putting some of the potatoes and gravy on as a condiment. Novel, as long as you could eat without wearing it.

Miguel's silk tie would somehow end up coated and probably ruined.

"There has been no news," Miguel began so that Dolf could chew. "I presume at this point that we are in a holding pattern of some sort until Segura decides to surface again? Or perhaps somebody finds his body and our informants at the police station quietly call?"

He desperately hoped that he hadn't sent Segura to his death at the hands of Esme, if she was the one trying to have the man killed. Nothing pointed at Stansfield so far except circumstantial evidence that would never stand up in a court proceeding.

Not that something like this would ever go beyond a star chamber headed by the Minister herself.

"That's correct," Dolf said after a quick swallow. "Protocol calls for a number of places he could leave us messages, but as he said, we've been compromised to some degree, although we didn't see anyone at the bakery."

"Would whoever it was have been warned to stay out of

your way?" Miguel asked as he scraped up the last of the pasta and ate it.

"Presumably," Dolf replied. "We've found the two handcomms that Rob's used so far, so I presume that he'll buy or steal a third one at some point. Maybe a fourth, if that becomes necessary. Alicia is watching all inbound traffic, with orders to immediately reach out to you or me if she hears from Rob."

"Will he go to ground?" Miguel asked.

Most operations were things he heard about well after the fact, reading a report and perhaps interviewing an agent for salient details that might not have made it onto the page. He'd rarely been in the middle of something actually going on, if only because the rare times something like that happened were usually arrests of double agents or attempted infiltrators.

The sorts of things that were handled quietly.

"I would," Dolf nodded grimly. "Find someplace to hide and let the hunters relax. Maybe reach out tomorrow. Or even just walk in the front door Monday and get inside the building before anybody realizes it."

"Who can he trust?" Miguel asked pointedly.

Dolf started to respond with heat, but bit the words back and took a bite of his sandwich as he reconsidered what he would say.

Not that Miguel would have held that sort of loyalty against Dolf, but things were not what they seemed, and Segura would have no idea who he could turn to.

Hopefully, Miguel had been safe in trusting Esme enough to use her as a bridge. There was no way Miguel could tell if her message was coerced, except that Segura wouldn't know the meaning of the code phrases she used, so he couldn't translate.

Right now, she was the only one Miguel could truly rely

on, if only because anything that happened to Handsome Rob would reflect badly on her otherwise. It was almost imperative that she get the man to safety, because failure might blow her cover.

If she was the insider with the leak.

It could still be Dillon. Or Dolf. Or Stansfield. Or a dozen others.

"I don't know," Dolf finally opined after swallowing. "We need to run a counter-intelligence sweep of the building, but we do those regularly enough already that whoever might be our mole has found a way around them. If I had a way to get a message to Rob without everyone knowing, I'd walk out the front door right now and meet him. Find a way to bring him in that protected him."

"Let's turn the heat down, then, instead of up," Miguel said quietly.

"Down?" Dolf was shocked.

"Yes, down," Miguel repeated. "Feed the local police a cover story about any shooting that got reported. Claim it was one of our training programs and somebody forgot to inform them. Blame the explosion on something other than terrorism if asked. Pull all your teams back into the building itself and stand them mostly down, rather than having them out where they can respond to anything in minutes."

"Is that wise?" Dolf asked. "We've got hunters out there. We need to chase them down."

"We don't know who they are," Miguel said. "Nothing can really happen right now until we hear from Segura, and he needs to feel safe enough to contact us. He can't do that if there are armed teams randomly moving around."

Dolf sat and considered it for a few moments before he finally nodded.

"Do we send most of the current staff home and bring in

a second group?" Dolf asked in a much lower voice. "Perhaps we get lucky and everyone who remains is safe?"

"Worth taking the risk," Miguel smiled tightly.

Dolf stuffed the last bite into his mouth and chewed mightily.

Miguel could send Stansfield home, maybe. Tell the man that he would be needed to pull long shifts Sunday and perhaps Monday as they sorted everything out?

It wouldn't necessarily eliminate him as a suspect, unless Miguel decided to send Esme a message and see what happened at the other end, but he didn't know what was going on out in the field, and didn't dare send a message at the wrong moment.

For one wild moment, he considered heading home himself and leaving Dolf in command of the building. It might make sense, if Segura was going to disappear for a while.

Should he send Esmeralda an invitation to dinner? Would she arrived with one tired and slightly paranoid agent in tow?

Yes. He would do something completely out of character, if for no other reason than to throw off all the calculations made by whoever had probably presumed that they wouldn't be able to get Miguel Cabrill out of his office with dynamite.

"Let's assume quiet for now, then," Miguel said while Dolf was unable to reply. "I'll go home and send Stansfield as well. You'll be in charge until one of us returns. Since you don't expect to hear from Segura, that lets you reorganize staffing levels as well. Maybe we'll flush someone from cover. Or perhaps create an opening for our boy to make it home safely."

"If you think that's wise, Miguel," Dolf managed around a mouthful of meatloaf.

"Playing the odds, Dolf," he smiled. "Something Royo does quite well. Hoping something good comes of it."

He rose with his tray in hand and stepped to one side.

"Get Segura home safe," he said simply. "Everything else can take second place to that. Am I clear?"

"You are," Dolf said. "I just wish it didn't come down to that."

"And I, as well," Miguel said, moving away.

He could order Stansfield home if he himself left. Long watch schedules waiting for an agent to return made a reasonable excuse, if Stansfield would need to take over the Operations Center at midnight, so Dolf could sleep, having been up and running like hell all day.

Meanwhile, desk-bound Miguel Cabrill would pretend to act like a field agent.

How desperate have we become?

32

Rob wasn't that engrossed in the movie, but it had enough noise and light to keep him from falling asleep. More of a romantic comedy than an action flick, although it had elements of both.

He just didn't like the implications of the casting and plot.

Bad boy thief accidentally meets good girl lawyer. Several rounds of fish out of water scenes followed by the usual romantic hijinks. He could see the ending coming a kilometer away. They followed a formula so ancient that Homer probably wrote it at some point.

At the time they'd walked into the theater, it had been the next movie showing, other than the teen slasher that would wind him up in all the wrong ways, since that was pretty much his morning already.

Mac stirred, next to him. They weren't holding hands in the theater. His verisimilitude only went so far, especially in the dark. He glanced over and saw her pull her handcomm from her inside jacket pocket, open it, and read a message.

He was at the wrong angle to see the words, but he stirred, ignoring the film.

A moment later, Mac turned the screen so he could see it, holding it for him to take the device.

Message from Miguel Cabrill. Head of the Service itself. Her boss. Everyone's boss.

Do you have dinner plans?

Simple enough. Rob wondered if it was one of the communication codes from her file.

He looked up at her. Leaned close enough to whisper in her ear.

"Code?" he asked.

"No," she whispered back. "Occasionally I have dinner with him and Caroline. Can't imagine him doing that in the middle of all this. Nothing deeper that I'm aware of."

Rob nodded. It was out of character for that man. He didn't know if that made it better or worse. Cabrill was notorious for staying in his office, reading reports and drawing people into his lair to get their brains emptied onto his desk.

Handsome Rob had gone through it twice now, both times the *Can't Shoot Straight Gang* had pulled a caper, but he'd just been sitting to one side while Jorge explained things.

Assuming the woman wasn't lying about the Director in the first place, maybe he was setting himself up as a target to bring Rob in? That was the only spin that made any sense at all.

"May I?" Rob asked, rather than just assuming.

"Go ahead," she said quietly.

Rob typed.

Dinner plans already. Drinks later?

Why the hell not?

He handed her the device and blew out a breath. Was there anything stupider than to just show up at the man's house and expect the Director to bring out the good whiskey?

The handcomm buzzed in Mac's hands a few moments later. She snorted and handed it to him.

Capital. Bring a +1 if you can.

Ye Gods, the man was serious. They were just going to sit around in his salon and chat? How deep would the security forces be around the building when Mac called later?

But if Mac and the Director were behind all his troubles, he was up shit creek to begin with.

Did this mean that maybe someone had been identified as a suspect? That made more sense. Mac had said that she and the Director were personal friends, so maybe this was all a cover ruse to rescue a lost duckling who couldn't trust anyone else?

Someone reading that exchange would have to know that Mac had been sent out specifically to contact Handsome Rob.

How would Jorge handle it?

Audacity, in spaces. That was Jorge's signature.

Maybe he could roll up with Ahmed in tow, just to introduce him to the Director and maybe get some official coverage on the cop who was coloring well outside the lines tonight?

How stupid would he feel like getting afterwards, if they managed to take down this hit team? Rob couldn't imagine getting lucky enough to find clues to whoever had hired them.

No, more likely it would require forensic fraud accountants. Bankers expert at unraveling money trails.

If you knew where one rope ended, eventually you should be able to walk it all the way back to the other end, unless someone was smart enough to do everything in cash.

But then you had witnesses. People who would identify

you in a police lineup, or pull your picture from a file and tap it expertly.

Most likely credit transfers, laundered and filtered through a dozen intermediaries.

Those worked great if you were facing cops who had to get warrants at every step of the investigation, leaving the suspect time to flee if they had a sniff of trouble.

The Service existed because sometimes you had to break the rules.

Rob looked up and realized that Mac was staring at him.

"Audacity," he grinned.

"You're serious?" she whispered, a little aghast from the tone.

"I'm open to possibilities, Mac," he let the smile take hold. "I try not to get stodgy and set in my ways, because then you can't take advantage of fortuitous serendipity when it walks up and punches you in the mouth."

He handed her back the handcomm, and, just for the hell of it, took hold of her hand like they were two teenagers on a date.

He already knew that the movie ended happily. They always did.

Maybe Handsome Rob could survive all this stupidity, as well. And do it with a gun-toting babe next to him.

33

—————

DODGER STUDIED HIS WAREHOUSE FROM THE CAB OF A crane several blocks away. He and the team were over where big containers from shuttles or freighters could be lifted off haulers and put onto train cars to be moved around the planet.

Safe, hopefully.

It was Saturday afternoon now and the port generally ran a five-day week, which was nice. Shut down around here except for some security guards who weren't above a quick bribe, as long as Dodger and his team didn't start up the crane or touch anything.

He just needed the elevation to see every which way.

Nothing stood out, and there weren't many places to hide, if you were going to send the cops after them.

I mean, sure, you could just have one person with a good enough view, or a camera so tiny as to be invisible, and then call in a strike team, but there was almost nothing Dodger or the boys could do about that.

Unless maybe he needed to burn the person that had

175

hired them. But that was the paranoia talking, not the professionalism.

He had to remember not to let his dark voices get out of hand.

"Anybody see anything?" he asked, including Swede, down in the car on his comm, as well as the others up here.

Nobody did. Either an elaborate trap, or obsessive ravings in his head.

"Let's do it, then," he said simply.

Out the door to the stairwell down. Back and forth down the immense construct, until they made it to the ground and piled into the car. Out of the storage yard and up the side street that would take them to their grubby little warehouse.

Everyone had a gun in hand except Swede as the driver pressed the button and one of the three garage doors rolled silently up.

Now was when it got deadly.

Inside, nobody was waiting with badges and guns, thank the gods.

Everyone piled out and inspected things fast enough.

All of the windows at the top were covered over with a film that let diffused light in, but not watchers. The outer shell of the building was intact and dirty, but the interior had been finished off into a living space for six, with bedrooms that had attached baths, living area, kitchen, and storage.

Plus a shooting range along one wall that was insulated against sound to the point that everyone could stay sharp without ever having to appear on someone's range records.

Ghosts in the system. Rats hiding in the walls.

It had been a day, but Dodger didn't let everyone slack now.

"At least one gun on you at all times," he said loudly as everyone finished their sweep and ended up back in the living room. "Including when you go to bed, either under the pillow or on the side table."

Good natured grumbles, but that was to be expected. They'd been on for twelve hours now, and everyone needed some down time.

"How long?" Kovalchuk asked.

"We'll eat dinner at around six, and then reevaluate things," Dodger decided.

That gave everyone time to nap or play silly games on their handcomm. Whatever it took to decompress, so that they could go do this all again later.

A professional agent who was getting desperate would take the afternoon off to plan something for night. Easier for one man to be standing in an alley when a car drove up so they could get in. Hard to track.

Dodger had a private bet with himself that the target would not reach out to the Service folks again until nightfall. Catch his team up for twenty-four hours, constantly expect a go-call, and then too muddy to actually react when it came time later.

Still, they could be out the door in under five minutes, since nobody would take a shower right now and dinner would come out of the freezer and into a microwave.

Dodger found a comfortable spot on one of the couches and reviewed every step they had taken, from the moment that kicking in the target's door had failed, up until the car had pulled into the warehouse and the door closed.

Every step had been by the rules. Right down the line on how you were supposed to do it, including hiding more or less in plain sight while the other team of agents tried to look inconspicuous.

Had they been wrong, something bad would have happened by now.

But nothing accounted for the raw luck that the target

had displayed. Except that the first door had been so heavy that it had resisted a boot. And shooting the one lock had only revealed five more on the inside.

By the time they'd blown the damned thing off the hinges, the target had vanished.

Only because Swede had been patrolling at random had the target been spotted later.

This didn't feel like a punk kid agent, still wet behind the ears, regardless of what their principal had told them. The man had manufactured luck by being one step ahead of them.

Dodger didn't think he was being set up. If so, he would have expected the boom to drop on them at that bakery.

Still, he got up and walked to the front door of the warehouse, next to the two bay doors that opened, opposite the six that had been permanently sealed off from the inside.

Still locked.

He peeked through the hole and confirmed that nobody was outside sneaking up before he opened the door and knelt down to inspect the lock. No electronics here. Nothing that could be brute-forced open with enough time and a rude computer.

This required a seven-pin key to open. Custom and handmade, expensive as hell.

Useful when you didn't want even a professional thief to be able to get in.

The lock had no damage indicating someone had tried to open it with any tools. The wires around the frame were still intact when Dodger stood and inspected them. The house security system hadn't shown any breaks in coverage or transmission, so nobody had managed to get in and reset it, at least without resetting the entire system so successfully that it left no records.

Because if you could do that, why not just stand around

for thirty cops that all had guns pointed at the car when it rolled in.

Dodger grumbled under his breath as he closed the door again and set the lock and the interior deadbolt.

None of this felt right, but he couldn't say where it had gone wrong.

34

———

Rob let Mac drive. Hadn't even stolen her
skimmer at the last minute to prevent her from being here.

The parking lot was close enough to the final destination, but it was out of the way enough that no civilians might wander over to see what was going on, and the bad guys would have to go out of their way to see the spot.

"There," Rob pointed as he spotted Ahmed, clustered together with a group of folks in an open box formed by three vehicles parked together.

Mac handled the skimmer like a pro and closed the square off as the men in the middle watched, maybe a little apprehensively.

He looked over and studied her profile as she was shutting everything down. She glanced up at him.

"Last chance to back out," he said simply.

"No, I think you should come with us, Rob," she grinned at him. "It's your party, after all."

He grinned back at the woman. At this person she had become.

Mac had loosened up over the course of the afternoon.

Almost sounded human now when she talked. Her vocabulary and grammar had undergone a code-shift, so that she sounded more like the field agents he knew, rather than the analysts.

Hopefully a good sign.

Rob exited the vehicle and got a hug from Ahmed. Mac was offered a hand to shake, but she still wasn't wearing a bra and it was rather obvious if you stared.

Six other men surrounded them as Ahmed handed over a pair of headphones with microphones you swung into place and then a pair of pulse pistols in holsters. Class three, like Mac had requested.

Rob preferred a four, but could shoot anything.

"This is Rob and Mac," Ahmed introduced them. "It's his op."

Rob studied the men, surprised that the chest armor they were wearing didn't mark them as cops, but this wasn't an officially sanctioned thing, so they needed to be low profile. The faces were still hard.

Much more serious than just beat cops. The killers Ahmed had called when he needed a sub-rosa favor.

He decided to play on that.

"This morning, at oh-dark-thirty, a group of men tried to kick in my door to kill me," he announced simply. "I work for the *Guardia Civil Interior* as a spy, and somebody there doesn't like me. Mac also works for the Service. This is a private affair, however, and not an officially sanctioned assassination."

There. Remind them that folks like me do bad things occasionally to protect folks like you.

"I got a tag number off a vehicle later, and Ahmed was able to trace it for me," Rob continued. "I'm hoping that they're home right now, but I don't really expect to be able to arrest them if they are. Assume that they'll open fire as soon as we breach, and act accordingly. I will not be leading that team. If this works right, I'll be on the roof scouting for you. When you distract them, I'll come down a rope and hit them in a flank. There are four shooters and a driver on that team, all male, but you won't be able to identify who is which until we have them custody. There might be more than five people in the building. Again, I won't know until I scout. Questions?"

"Am I on the roof with you, or going in the front?" Mac asked, mostly as a cover.

They had already sorted it all out ahead of time. She'd never done the thing where you're free-falling on a line and have to shoot targets as they popped out at you, and this didn't seem like the best time for a first try.

"On the ground," Rob said. "I'll need maximum stealth up there if we're going to surprise them."

"How tough is the door?" one of the men asked.

"I would presume as hard as you can get," Rob said. "Nobody's seen the interior, but I've seen exterior shots, and there are two garage doors next to it. Do you have enough explosives handy that you could blow a couple of panels off their rails?"

"Actually, I was kinda planning on stealing a forklift and ramming the thing," Ahmed said sheepishly. "Never met a civilian garage door yet that was reinforced enough. Would use my own car, but I expect that they parked theirs just inside, so I'm likely to slam into the back of it at speed. Rather not."

Rob shook his head, but kept his opinion to himself. Ahmed wasn't a crooked cop, as far as Rob had been able to tell without asking someone like Mac to have run a background check on him at some point. But he supposed that there might be a forklift lying around that someone could hotwire if they needed to.

"Anybody else?" Rob asked.

The tough guys shook their heads. They'd need his intel to know what problems they faced.

He turned to look up at Ahmed.

"You've got the address," he said and the man nodded. "I'll have her drop me off nearby and then come back and join up with you. Expect that I'll need twenty minutes to get into position and ready for you, so go find your forklift and then meet up. Mac will show you where I want everybody staged for the raid."

Hard faces. Men prepared to go raid a den of bad guys because Ahmed had requested it on their day off, rather than everyone in uniforms with the Chief backing them up.

Hopefully, he wasn't getting everyone into more trouble than they could handle.

Rob nodded to everyone, and he and Mac climbed back into her skimmer.

He could already taste the coming violence.

35

———

ROB UNBUCKLED AS THE SKIMMER SETTLED, TWO
blocks away from the warehouse, down and around a corner.
He had Nigel's oversized goody bag with him.

"Good luck," Mac said simply.

He turned back from opening the door and nodded.
Again, in the movies, this was where the romantic interest
gave the hero a kiss for luck, but he didn't feel like pushing
his any farther right now than he already had.

"Be safe," he said instead. "Let Ahmed and his boys lead,
because they'll have had experience at it."

"Understood," she replied simply.

They'd talked after the movie, while getting emotionally
ready for this. Rob had spent three years preparing for
tonight. She'd spent three hours.

Nowhere near close to enough, but at least she knew
what was coming. Hopefully.

In his wildest fantasies, the men would all be napping
when he managed to get on the roof and look, and someone
could pick the lock, slip in quietly, and get the drop on them.

He didn't believe it for a second, but it made a nice

mental image.

Second best would be following Roxy through a door as she tried to set a new high score.

Rob watched the skimmer zip off, then he moved quickly to the corner to look around.

These warehouses were all reinforced concrete faced with brick, usually fifteen meters tall or so, with concrete shell roofs. Heavier than metal, but built to last for centuries. He could climb the brick. Had it been smooth, he'd have had to have someone drop him on the roof he wanted.

Not the best way to sneak up on someone, if only because he would have expected sensors up here to pick that up.

From the images he'd downloaded to his map, two sides of the warehouse were blank, with bay doors down one side and a pair of doors on what would be the front, if someone built the place out to have a shipping and receiving office.

Since the commercial port was mostly closed, there was little traffic this afternoon. It being dinner time, most of that had fallen to nothingness.

He crossed between buildings like a tourist, on the off chance that someone happened to be looking at a camera right now. Around to the back, to the farthest corner from the doors.

Rob looked both ways, but there was nobody about. He checked the pistol again, then pulled out the ninja climbing claws that Nigel had insisted on including for hands and boots. Rob had heard the story of Jorge hanging from the side of a building, waiting for a husband to leave, so he supposed that they worked.

Claws you could attach to your hand. Set them to the right angle and they'd hold the next brick above your fingers. All well and good.

Rob took a deep breath and began to climb, making sure

to stay away from the aluminium down spout that would catch rain runoff. Tempting to grab if he got in trouble, but they weren't ever attached worth a damn, and would just make a tremendous noise if he started to fall and grabbed that instead.

At least these bricks were real, rather than a facia board. Solid, like a mountain, with the mortar inset enough that he could get a solid grip as he moved. Almost like free-climbing, but that wasn't a hobby Rob had ever felt like taking up.

Roof.

He let go a breath and pulled himself over the ledge.

No obvious sensors visible. About a five degree pitch to the roof down the long axis. Skylights about every ten meters, each about a half meter tall and meter and a half square. Enough to let a breeze in on a hot day and suck heat out if they were open.

And nobody running around a corner with a gun to shoot him.

Always a plus.

Rob assumed that the front of the warehouse would probably be the living quarters. You'd park in the equivalent of a garage, and walk into the kitchen, like most homes with an attached parking structure. He moved along the outer edge, peeking over occasionally to see what might be going on below.

At least there were no doorways on the roof where an internal staircase might let someone jump out and shoot him.

The sun was mostly hidden at this point, leaving that gray, hazy evening that you got this time of year. The roof was a little slick from earlier, but not bad. He could see a glow below four of the skylights as he approached, so he hoped he had guessed right.

They were filmed over, as he had expected. You wanted

the ambient light, but didn't necessarily want someone to do exactly what Rob was about to attempt.

He reached into the bag and pulled out a camera and a drill. When he quietly tapped the skylight, it was plastic, rather than glass, so that made it easier to work. The plastic might just be opaque.

Nigel was a sneaky bastard. Rob set the tiny drill in place at a corner of the plastic and lowered a shroud that somehow muffled the sound as he pulled the trigger and the hollow bit began to bore its way through.

Quickly, he had a hole too small for even Mac's pinky to fit, but enough. He slipped the drill back into the bag and lined his teeny camera up.

The thing slipped into the hole and rested on a flange all the way around, tiny and hopefully invisible.

Rob pulled out a set of goggles and leaned back to watch inside the warehouse below, controlling things with a roller next to his left eye.

Garage door. Ground vehicle he'd photographed earlier. Vehicle maintenance bay.

Next to that, beyond a three meter tall wall like a movie set, a kitchen and dining area, with a rec room/salon beyond that. A row of rooms with roofs that Rob assumed must be bedrooms, so someone could snore and not keep the team awake.

Looking around, maybe a couple of internal shooting galleries, from the length and shape. Lots of extra space that had never been developed, mostly in shadow, but without cover of any kind.

Rob dialed the camera back to the dining room.

Five men. Hard to identify them from above, but the number was promising. Two were already eating. One was supervising a microwave. One was digging in the refrigerator. The last one was stirring something on the stove.

Okay, dinner time for the team. Maybe they came home after lunch and napped or something. Getting themselves all set for another evening's romp, once they got a call from someone.

He couldn't see any alcohol on the table or any of the places he looked. Water. Maybe juice. Maybe tea. Ah, coffee maker with a carafe next to the stove.

"Two, this is one," Rob said quietly into the microphone.

"Two. Go ahead," Ahmed replied a moment later.

"In the front door there is a short hallway with a bathroom and maybe a pantry," Rob said. "Through that you are in a kitchen, with the dining room beyond that in a straight line. I have eyes on five men cooking or eating. If you come in through the garage, you'll have to come through a doorway on the left that separates things. Think movie set. Salon beyond dining room, then bedrooms. Lots of space in the darkness beyond that, but nowhere to hide behind something."

"Are they prepared for shooting?" Mac asked on the line.

"Negative, but I doubt it would take them long," Rob said. "Can you breach the door and garage at the same time?"

"Affirmative, one," another voice came over the line. "How long do you need to prepare?"

"Probably three minutes," Rob guessed. "Will advise when I'm ready."

"Roger that."

Rob popped the goggles up onto his forehead and rooted around in Nigel's medicine bag of goodies. Rope and grapple that could be deployed. He set it in place and unwound the rope into a loose coil to one side.

The skylight itself was a low pyramid, four seams coming up to a point about fifteen centimeters higher than the edges. Just enough to keep rain and dirt off it.

Nigel had packed a small amount of a thermal

compound. It was overkill for a skylight like this, but there were no points for neatness in this situation. He was more or less over the center of the rec room right now, so if he was lucky, he'd catch them facing the other direction. However, the sound of the skylight falling to the deck would draw all eyes his way.

Too bad Nigel hadn't included a couple of stun grenades. He'd have to have a chat with the man about that for next time.

Assuming that he'd have to go through this level of stupidity again.

Rob climbed into an abseiling harness and attached the rope. Put everything away except the detonator control for the breaching charge. Slung Nigel's messenger bag out of his way.

Drew the pistol and flipped the safety off. Pulled the goggles down just long enough that he could see what was going on inside.

"Two, this is one," he said, taking a deep breath. "At your convenience."

Rob heard a sound that his brain interpreted as a forklift burning a petroleum-based fuel, getting up to speed. A moment later, the sound of a symphony of anvils being tossed down a staircase washed over him.

Then something exploded. Like someone blowing a lock off a door.

Rob pulled the goggles down around his neck and counted to three.

He closed his eyes and pressed the switch to set up the heat charge.

The whole roof shuddered as the skylight fell inward.

Rob tossed the rope into the hole, took a breath, and leaped.

36

———

MAC WATCHED THE MEN AROUND HER PREPARE. LOW murmurs. Tense hands. Nervous eyes glancing over at her occasionally.

But she was the unknown. A spy. Maybe an assassin. Certainly trouble.

Mac didn't bother correcting these men, as she'd spent twenty-five years behind an electronics console, fighting her wars with security systems and communications protocols.

Ahmed was driving a stolen forklift with the rails removed. Two other men had attached something to the door and turned their faces away.

She was off to the other side with the remaining three.

"At your convenience," Rob said over the line.

Ahmed smiled and got a running start at the garage door. Mac closed her eyes, expecting a flash of blinding light shortly.

Ahmed had been right. The door was basically fiberglass, rather than steel, and shattered like an egg when he hit it.

The others set off whatever explosives they had planted, and the other door shattered inward with a bang.

The forklift had slammed squarely into the back of a late model sedan and stopped, but the three men in front of Mac had gone right around it, guns up and moving quickly.

She kept expecting them to yell *Police, nobody move*, but they remained silent.

Somewhere off to her left, a pulse pistol fired. Something heavier responded.

Her three men moved to the kitchen door, firing.

Rob had said that the place was a movie set, so she shifted to a place where the wall looked like simple gypsum board and smiled. In a building fire, people often died because they got trapped in a room, never realizing that they could take a chair and bash their way through interior walls fast enough.

The pulse beams from the kitchen grew more intense.

Mac didn't want to jump into the middle of a firefight, but she could help.

Two quick pulses shattered a spot on the wall in front of her. She reached a gloved hand in and pulled insulation out of the way. Two more shots and the wall was suddenly exploding outward in a circle as big as her chest.

Mac leaned and fired at movement, catching at least one man from behind with surprise.

Crossfire.

Someone else panicked and started raking the wall, so she leaned back and found the stud on her left. It wouldn't do much to stop pulse fire, but every shot sent this way was one not engaging the policemen on her left.

37

Rob fell into the space below. Nobody was looking his way, and he didn't want to start himself spinning by firing, so he just concentrated on falling and then grabbed the rope hard when he was about three meters in the air.

All hell was breaking loose over there, so he wanted to be on the ground fast, since he was more or less in line with cops coming in the front door.

Someone had flipped a table onto the side and was using that as cover. Rob got to the floor, squatted, and detached his line before he bothered taking a potshot at the men in the kitchen. There was a sofa, so he rolled to his right.

Wouldn't stop pulse fire, but it would make it harder to hit him.

Screams of rage and surprise.

And pain.

Pulse fire everywhere.

Rob leaned out and shot one man that had turned sideways and was spraying the wall randomly.

As that man went down, he realized that the shadow he saw was Mac on the other side. She seemed to be smiling.

Fire dropped so suddenly Rob was shocked.

"I surrender," a man yelled in pain.

Rob oozed around the side of the sofa.

Mac was peeking from behind her pistol through the hole she had blasted in the wall

The kitchen was a complete mess. Food-fight-in-the-quad level mayhem.

Four men down. Maybe not dead yet, because pulse fire tended to rupture rather than punch holes in fragile bodies.

One man more or less on his ass against the refrigerator, holding his right shoulder with his left hand. That was the one who'd wanted to talk turkey.

"Ahmed, coming from cover," Rob yelled, just so nobody shot him accidentally.

"All clear," the cop replied.

Mac winked at him and then disappeared from sight.

He'd never considered coming *through* a wall to get to someone. Needed to remember that trick.

Lord knows, he didn't figure this would be the last time he had to shoot someone.

Bodies everywhere, but only two of them looked outright dead. One of Ahmed's guys was a medic, apparently, and was treating one of the downed crooks, so maybe they would be able to arrest people.

Ahmed had stripped the one guy of weapons and everything by the time Rob and Mac got close.

Rob recognized him from the photo. Not the shooter or the spotter, but one of the men in back. The one that looked like he was in charge.

"Who are you?" the man asked through gritted teeth as four pistols were leveled at him.

"Just a guy," Rob replied. "Who the hell are you people, and what the hell did I do to you?"

"Nothing personal, mate," the man said. "This was just a job. We were hired to kill you and be done with it."

"Ahmed, I need to call for an ambulance," the medic piped up. "I think we can save these two, if we get them there fast enough."

Ahmed turned to Rob with an expectant look.

Rob approached the one prisoner. Squatted down to get close. Looked him in the eyes.

"You wanna just go to prison for a while?" Rob asked. "Be treated like a simple criminal thug?"

"What's the alternative?" the man asked.

"I shoot you and your buddies right now," Rob smiled. "Wouldn't be the first time I've done that with someone that wanted to be tough."

"What do you want to know?" he asked.

"One, what's your name?" Rob said. "Two, who hired you?"

"Name's Dodger," he said. "Got no idea who hired us. Came through the usual channels and third party fixer."

Mac suddenly squatted down on Dodger's other side, holding the man's handcomm.

"Tell me the code to open it, and we might make you a deal, Dodger," she said. "I'm a senior agent with the Service. If you play us straight, and haven't been lying, maybe we can use you later."

Dodger turned to study the woman closely.

"There's nothing on there that's incriminating," he said.

"Then you have nothing to fear," Mac smiled. "Or my friend here can shoot you. Your choice."

"Six-four-nine-one," he said.

Rob watched her key the code and open the handcomm. She nodded at him and stood.

Rob smiled at Dodger.

"You play me straight, and I'll reciprocate," he said.

Rob stood and looked at Ahmed.

"If you take them in and book them on possession of illegal firearms, you ought to be able to hold them quiet for a few days," he said. "This will be resolved by then."

"What about you?" Ahmed asked.

Rob glanced down at Dodger and then over at Mac.

"We were never here," he said, turning and walking towards the door.

38

IT FELT BACKWARDS, BUT MAC MADE ROB GET IN THE driver's seat while she worked on Dodger's handcomm.

"Where are we going, anyway?" the man asked as he put the vehicle in motion.

Mac suddenly realized that she still had Ahmed's pistol, but it was probably too late to give it back. Maybe she'd swing by that bar some Saturday and see if he was in. Or Rob could return it.

"Do you know where Miguel lives?" she asked.

Rob looked at her with surprise.

"I was just kidding when I said that earlier."

"Well it's probably a good idea at this point," she countered.

"How's that?" Rob asked, still not starting forward.

"This handcomm is remarkably similar to the ones we issue to agents," she explained. "Like yours that went to the vegetable market this morning."

"Okay?"

"So none of the contacts have actual names attached," she said. "Just what looks like contract numbers, if I had to guess. Maybe Dodger's filing system. When Ahmed turns the place over later, I'll need to put one of my teams in there to crack all Dodger's files and see who else has hired him over the years, assuming he has enough data handy."

"Still not following," Rob said.

"Drive," she said, giving him the actual address to the old part of town, near the university, where Miguel and Caroline lived. "So the most recent set of calls in and out today have to be Dodger talking to the person who hired him."

"Makes sense," Rob agreed, finally lifting the skimmer up on the repulsors and pulling into the street. "So we can track them down that way?"

"We don't need to," Mac said. "I recognize the number. I set it up originally."

"Do you have an eidetic memory, or something?" He glanced over.

"Yes," Mac said, watching the blood drain out of his face.

Every man got twitchy at the moment they realized that everything they had ever said could be repeated back to them later, word for word. For most people, it made them back well off, lest they expose themselves too much.

Only a few had the intelligence to just not tell her lies that they could be caught in later.

"Suppose I'll need to be more careful what I say to you in the future," his seriousness dissolved into a smile.

She smiled back. That presupposed that the man would talk to her again after all this was done.

Was she in favor of that?

He was a playboy in the mode and under the tutelage of Jorge Royo, so there was always that to pay attention to. At the same time, an exceedingly small number of women or men had ever found a reason to complain about Royo. And none about Segura, at least to date. But he was still young, not quite twenty-eight yet, and she felt ancient at fifty-one.

"So do we trust Cabrill?" Handsome Rob asked, seriousness returning.

"We do," Mac decided. "I suspect that it will be something of a shock to the man, when he hears the truth, but he wouldn't have sent me out to rescue you, had he known."

"Who's the leak?" Rob asked. "Dolf got it in for me, in spite of everything else?"

"No," Esmeralda MacTavish said. "Apparently Stansfield Brightmeadow-Gates does."

39

─────

MIGUEL OPENED THE DOOR WITH A MOMENT OF trepidation. He'd sent Caroline out to stay with her sister for the evening, just so that if anything untoward were to happen to him, she'd be safe.

Everyone had their own flavor of cowardice.

On the porch, slightly in shadow, a pair of figures waited as the echoes of the Westminster chimes faded away.

Had he not known what to expect, Miguel might have never known who the two strangers on his stoop were. Esme looked barely past her teenage years, somehow, and the man with her carried himself with the heavy seriousness that most men didn't learn until they were past forty.

Miguel stepped to one side and gestured them in.

"Quickly now," he said, closing the door after they were passed.

Yes, Esme had a vitality about her Miguel hadn't seen before. And Segura looked more like Royo describing the ugly elements of free-lance improvisation that happened when a mission went sideways.

"Come," he said, walking past them and not taking jackets, since he wasn't sure how long they'd be there.

Into the kitchen, where he'd drawn the shades enough to protect them from outside observation. Just in case, he'd left one of Esme's hand scanners on the counter, in case she needed to sweep the place again.

Like he'd done every fifteen minutes since he got home.

Everyone had their own flavor of paranoia, too.

Rather than play the genial host with welcome guests, Miguel went to the counter and poured himself a highball of the good whiskey. He'd teetotaled all afternoon, lest he dull his wits at the moment he needed them sharp. Come to think of it, this bottle had been a present from Royo.

Miguel sat at one of the barstools and watched.

"Fix yourself drinks, if you will," he said pointedly. "Esme, you know where everything is."

Segura poured himself just enough whiskey in a matching glass to perhaps toast with, but not even a mouthful. Esme did the same.

Segura pulled his own scanner out and ran it around the room, but nothing beeped untoward.

"How bad is it?" Miguel asked, confronted by a hunted agent in his own kitchen, and his Director of the Data Analysis Inspectorate, looking like an assassin.

"Rob's safe," Esme said. "The team that had been hunting him has been eliminated."

Miguel nearly dropped his glass.

"Eliminated?"

"Neutralized is perhaps a better term," she continued. "Two maybe dead at the scene. Three wounded to various degrees, but the medic thought that they could possibly all be saved. They are in police custody at present and being kept from communications with the outside world."

"How?" Miguel asked, feeling the world sway

unexpectedly under his feet.

Rather than answer, Esme turned to Segura.

"I called in some favors," Segura answered in a tone that wasn't going to offer suggestions. "Mac here tells me that she's solved the case, and we needed to move quickly to arrest the ringleader."

Mac?

Good heavens, what had happened this afternoon and this evening? And where had these strange beings come from?

"Ringleader?" Miguel finally managed. "Who?"

"Stansfield," Esme said in as definitive a tone as Segura's. "We got the handcomm from the leader of the team by promising him leniency."

"Leniency?" Miguel felt his scruff rise in spite of everything. "For a killer? Why would you do that?"

"Because it was my fight," Segura snapped. "My decision."

"And the alternative wasn't one Dodger was willing to face," Esme said.

No, better make that *Mac*, whoever she was. Certainly not the woman he had sent out like bait ten hours ago.

"Which was?" Miguel demanded.

"I'd have just shot them out of hand," *Handsome Rob's* face wasn't attractive right now. "Put them down like mad dogs. This is Dodger's chance to maybe roll over to the right people and do jail time instead, if he can't convince you to hire him."

"Why would I do that?"

"They aren't bad agents," Segura said. "I got exceedingly lucky, and Jorge and Nigel are more paranoid than you are, Cabrill. Otherwise, I'd be dead. If they check out, you have a team of mercenaries. At least the ones that survive. And Dodger can always recruit more if the other two don't."

Miguel drank the rest of his whiskey for that cold burn

that would center his being a little better.

"So you think Stansfield is the bad apple?" he asked, putting the other matter to one side for now, but not forgetting it.

They could deal with that tomorrow. Field agents didn't make policy. They just made the best of worst-case choices in the middle of firefights.

"I do," Mac said. "And I'm pretty sure how to prove it to your satisfaction."

"How?"

"Give us twenty minutes as a head start," Mac said, glancing over at Segura for a nod. "Then contact Dolf and Stansfield and tell them that they both need to come in immediately."

"Dolf's already there," Miguel said. "Stansfield was due to relieve him on the Ops desk at midnight, if we hadn't heard from you before that, Segura."

"Even better," Mac smiled. "We'll sneak into the building. You summon Stansfield from home, and get him and Dolf into your office. We'll confront them then and there."

"You doubt Dolf?" Miguel demanded hotly.

"I doubt everybody, including you," Segura growled. "If Brightmeadow-Gates is going down alone, fine. But if he has help, I want them down at the same time."

"Fine," Miguel said in a snappish voice he couldn't help. "I can work with that. Did you have any other orders?"

"No."

Segura finished his splash of whiskey with a smile and set the glass down at the same time that this Mac person did. Both turned and headed towards the door in complete silence.

"Handsome. Mac," Miguel said as they did, causing both of them to pause and look back. "Good job."

40

MIGUEL WAS BACK AT HIS DESK, FILES PILED LIKE battlements. Midnight was approaching the outside of his fortress. He keyed the intercom.

"Ben, have our guests arrived?" he asked simply.

"Affirmative, Director," the young man chirped brightly, also back on the battlefield.

Life in the Service sometimes meant Saturday nights suddenly called back to the office with little warning, but the young man was nearly worth his weight in platinum. Miguel would miss his competence, when he decided he wanted to transfer to one of the other departments.

"Have Dolf and Stansfield come up for a briefing," Miguel said, letting go of the button.

Two chairs. A pile of file folders. His predecessor had kept a live firearm in the top drawer, but that fellow had come up from Operations, and truly deserved to be called a *Cowboy*.

Miguel preferred to handle things in a more bureaucratic manner. Even when he had to send Operations off the reservation to handle things.

He paused and waited, aware of wheels turning and Rube Goldberg balls rolling down tracks in unexpected, twisting ways.

What would the Service look like on Monday? Certainly, the coming investigations would be painful and torturous. Hopefully they could contain the cancer with surgery and a little chemotherapy, rather than having to burn the house down and start over.

He'd grow bored in retirement, regardless of how many times he had told Caroline he looked forward to that date.

Stansfield arrived first. Impeccably dressed, as always, with a red, striped tie running down at an angle to his left hip and offsetting the blue of his suit.

"News, Miguel?" he asked.

"Indeed," Miguel forced a smile, wondering all the while if the man had a weapon on him. "Just waiting for Dolf so I don't have to explain it twice."

"Very good," the undertaker took his seat primly and waited.

Dolf had to come up from Three, and was still dressed as before, ready to go into the field on a moment's notice, in casual dungarees, T-shirt, and flannel jacket.

The contrast between the two could not be more plain.

Dolf closed the door and took his seat.

"So I have been contacted by Segura," Miguel said. "Via outside channels that I believe were still secure enough to warrant trusting them."

It was educational, watching Dolf's eyes light up with happiness, while Stansfield somehow grimaced and glowered at the same instant, before shutting everything back down to utter neutrality so bland that his suit looked exotic by comparison.

"He's safe?" Dolf asked excitedly. "When can we get him home?"

"Ben has the information," Miguel said guilelessly. He keyed the intercom. "Benjamin, could you join us please?"

"Right away, sir," his assistant said.

Yes, he would miss the young man when he had to promote him for such cheerful competence.

The door opened. Both Dolf and Stansfield looked back over their inner shoulders and did a double take when Segura was standing there with a pistol in one hand, pointed negligently at the room.

The look on the agent's face was so cold that Miguel wished he had some coffee right now. Handsome Rob looked like a cook about to bone a chicken, rather than a Field Agent.

As Segura stepped into the room, Mac stepped up next to him, leaving Ben as a witness on the other side.

"Please don't anybody make me shoot you," Handsome announced in a flat, chicken-boning voice.

"What the hell's going on?" Dolf demanded, utterly still otherwise.

"Retribution," Mac said in a voice perhaps a shade colder than Rob's, if that was possible.

She pulled a handcomm from the pocket of her jacket and pressed a button. Immediately, Stansfield's pocket buzzed and the man jumped as if an electric circuit had closed.

Miguel was all set to have the man arrested, when Handsome Rob stepped up and cold-cocked Stansfield Brightmeadow-Gates so hard the man pitched out of his chair and collapsed bonelessly against the bookcase.

Dolf had started to stand, but Rob turned, that pistol still ready to shoot.

Dolf froze and looked up at Mac and Handsome Rob. Then at Ben. Then Stansfield.

Finally, he turned to look at Miguel, worry carved into his face with a welding laser, perhaps.

"What just happened?" he asked in a brittle voice. "Was that necessary?"

"That was what you get for hunting Handsome Rob," Miguel smiled.

ABOUT THE AUTHOR

Blaze Ward writes science fiction in the Alexandria Station universe (Jessica Keller, The Science Officer, The Story Road, etc.) as well as several other science fiction universes, such as Star Dragon, the Dominion, and more. He also writes odd bits of high fantasy with swords and orcs. In addition, he is the Editor and Publisher of *Boundary Shock Quarterly Magazine*. You can find out more at his website www.blazeward.com, as well as Facebook, Goodreads, and other places.

Blaze's works are available as ebooks, paper, and audio, and can be found at a variety of online vendors. His newsletter comes out regularly, and you can also follow his blog on his website. He really enjoys interacting with fans, and looks forward to any and all questions—even ones about his books!

Never miss a release!
If you'd like to be notified of new releases, sign up for my newsletter.

I will never spam you or use your email for nefarious purposes. You can also unsubscribe at any time.

http://www.blazeward.com/newsletter/

Connect with Blaze!

Web: www.blazeward.com
Boundary Shock Quarterly (BSQ):
https://www.boundaryshockquarterly.com/

ABOUT KNOTTED ROAD PRESS

Knotted Road Press fiction specializes in dynamic writing set in mysterious, exotic locations.

Knotted Road Press non–fiction publishes autobiographies, business books, cookbooks, and how–to books with unique voices.

Knotted Road Press creates DRM–free ebooks as well as high–quality print books for readers around the world.

With authors in a variety of genres including literary, poetry, mystery, fantasy, and science fiction, Knotted Road Press has something for everyone.

Knotted Road Press
www.KnottedRoadPress.com